D0816513

DRACONIAN NEW YORK

By Robert Sheckley
from Tom Doherty Associates, Inc.

The Alternative Detective
Draconian New York
Immortality, Inc.

DRACONIAN NEW YORK

ROBERT SHECKLEY

A TOM DOHERTY ASSOCIATES BOOK
NEW YORK

This is a work of fiction. All the characters and events portrayed in this novel are either fictitious or are used fictitiously.

DRACONIAN NEW YORK

This book is printed on acid-free paper.

Edited by David G. Hartwell

A Forge Book
Published by Tom Doherty Associates, Inc.
175 Fifth Avenue
New York, NY 10010

Forge® is a registered trademark of Tom Doherty Associates, Inc.

Library of Congress Cataloging-in-Publication Data

Sheckley, Robert, date
Draconian New York / by Robert Sheckley.
p. cm.
"A Tom Doherty Associates book."
ISBN 0-312-85130-8
1. Private investigators—New York (N.Y.)—Fiction.
I. Title
PS3569.H392D68 1996
813'.54—dc20 95-53234

First edition: July 1996

Printed in the United States of America

0 9 8 7 6 5 4 3 2 1

To my wife, Gail, with all my love

1

This whole thing began with the *traspaso,* so we might as well begin there, on a fine-looking day in Ibiza in late spring. Ibiza had many fine-looking days and this was one of the best of them: deep blue sky with a couple of puffy white clouds to give it character; brilliant sun filtering through the branches of the almond trees. The big old farmhouse with its solid white-washed walls. The grape arbor just visible through the little arch that led to the paved courtyard. A day to make you glad you were alive. And Hob Draconian was lying outside in dappled shadow in the Peruvian hammock he had bought at the hippie market in Punta Arabi.

He was just getting nicely relaxed when he saw something move in the distance. He sat up and saw two men walking among his almond trees. He got out of the hammock and stared at them. They were small figures in the distance, wearing dark suits, walking slowly, and talking to each other. One of them carried an aluminum clipboard that glinted in the sunlight, the other had a large briefcase. They both wore sunglasses.

Hob got out of the hammock, slipped on his sandals, and went out to see what they wanted. He usually didn't get trespassers in mid-June, this early in the season. He supposed they were a couple of foreigners, English or French, no doubt, unaware that you didn't walk across private land in Ibiza without first getting the owner's permission.

They saw him coming and waited for him. They were in their mid-thirties, Spanish, by the look of them, *peninsulares,* not islanders, and not a bit discomfited at being told they were trespassing on private land.

The one with the clipboard was tall and thin, with dark wavy hair. He said, "It is our information that this land is for sale."

"No, you've got that wrong," Hob said pleasantly. "This is my land and I'm not interested in selling."

The two Spaniards talked to each other in rapid Spanish. Then the first one said, "You have a deed to this land?"

"I have a *traspaso,*" Hob said. "And how is it any business of yours?"

"I am Lawyer Molinez," the tall, thin one with the clipboard said. "This is Architect Fernandez." He gestured at his shorter, thickset companion, who made a little nod of his head in acknowledgment. "We have been hired to look over your land and determine its suitability for our buyer."

"But I told you, this land is not for sale."

"You are not the owner," Molinez pointed out. He tapped the clipboard. "You are the renter. We have the permission of the owner."

"You mean Don Esteban?"

"Don Esteban's family."

"You must have made a mistake," Hob said. "You've gotten the wrong piece of land."

The architect Fernandez opened his briefcase and took out a survey map of Ibiza. Both men looked at it. Then the lawyer Molinez said, "No, this is the one. The landmarks are unmistakable."

"But I tell you, I have a *traspaso.* No one can sell this land."

"We understand that you have a *traspaso,*" Molinez said. "But we also understand that it expires soon."

"I have an understanding with Don Esteban. We have our own arrangement."

"That is not my information," Molinez said. "You have not

paid the principal sum on your *traspaso*. It falls due in less than a month. Our understanding is that the land is available for sale after"—he consulted his papers—"the fifteenth of July."

"This is a misunderstanding," Hob said. "I'll clear it up myself with Don Esteban. Meanwhile, now is June, not July. Please get off my land immediately."

"We are not harming anything," Molinez said. "We are merely surveying it in accord with the wishes of the people who will be the new owners."

"You're disturbing my tranquillity," Hob said. "Get out of here or I'll call the Guardia."

The Spaniards looked at each other and shrugged. "You would do better to be more cooperative. The new owners are prepared to offer you compensation for early evacuation."

"Get out!" Hob shouted. And the two Spaniards left.

Hob's house was called C'an Poeta. He had been living in it for about five years, ever since his arrival on the island, renting it from old Don Esteban, who owned C'an Poeta and several other properties. Hob and the old man had hit it off from the first time they met. Don Esteban dearly loved a game of chess down at the outdoor Kiosko Café in Santa Eulalia, under the big oak tree, over a glass of the rough red wine of the island. Chess was a skill he had picked up working on foreign vessels during his years away from the island.

He and Hob would often take long walks together, the old man sometimes carrying a bird gun but rarely shooting anything. The walks provided an opportunity for a bit of a ramble and (on Don Esteban's part) a bit of philosophizing about the never fading pleasures of nature. Nature is especially pretty in Ibiza and easily stands up to rhapsodizing. If your finca were in the chilly wastelands of the Ahaggar Mountains of Morocco you might tend to shy away from likening nature to a good-smelling all-supporting mother. But this figure of speech, a favorite of Don Esteban's, seemed proper and easy to support in Ibiza.

Hob always did have a weak side for nature rhapsodizing. It was what led him to hang out with hippies and third worlders in the first place. With them but never of them. And he always eventually tired of the hippies' air of self-conscious exaltation. It was part of what prevented Hob from ever being a successful flower child, though he tried from time to time. His good sense could always be counted on to return at some point, at which time he would, perhaps regretfully, take the flowers out of his hair and get on with whatever his life had been up to that time.

Buying and selling property on Ibiza is no small thing. There's always a drama involved. Don Esteban said he would be delighted to sell to Hob. He had come to think of him as a son, even if Hob's Spanish was poor and his Catalan nonexistent; more of a son to him than the two big louts who lived in his house and weren't interested in farming but in chasing foreign women and making deals, and who borrowed money from Don Esteban to spend at the dog track and the bar in the rifle club and the restaurant in the yacht club, places where the sons of well-to-do Ibicencans lived their own version of la dolce vita.

Traspaso is the arrangement by which a property in Spain is bought and sold. It's like a mortgage, only with Latin peculiarities. The islanders didn't think much of the *traspaso* system and tended to make their own informal arrangements, thus avoiding taxes and other official unpleasantries. When Hob had expressed an interest in buying C'an Poeta, property prices on the island had been low. Don Esteban had agreed to sell for the peseta equivalent of sixty thousand dollars. For that price, Hob got the house and 4.5 hectares of land on the north coast of the island. His small monthly rent had been put toward the purchase price. Hob didn't even know how much he still owed. But he and Don Esteban had an arrangement. Although legally Hob owed certain sums on certain dates, informally Don Esteban had assured him the place was his as long as he was alive and wanted it. After Hob's death, if the *traspaso* had not been exercised, the property would revert back to the Esteban family.

The old man was as good as his word. He drew up a document and a sum was agreed upon to bind it. Dates were solemnly decided and noted. This over little silver cups of Don Esteban's prize *hierbas,* made from twenty-one herbs picked at the correct times of the moon and steeped in white anisette, all this from a recipe that had been in the family for generations. But what they signed in the end after the lawyers got through with it was the standard house-selling lease in Spain as provided by Don Esteban's attorney, Hernan Matutes, who ran most of his practice from the back room of the Bar Balear on the promenade in Ibiza City.

Hob and the old man knew the agreement between them was solely for the purpose of providing legal protection in case of the old man's sudden death, which he wasn't expecting but thought he should safeguard against anyhow. Hob and Don Esteban were playing by the vaguely understood rules of a sense of honor which they felt in each other's presence. Hob would pay what he could when he could, that was the gist of the private agreement; and if he fell into arrears, well, no one cared!

"What's the matter?" Harry Hamm asked Hob that evening when they met at El Caballo Negro, the bar in Santa Eulalia where most of the foreign community got its mail.

"I had a run-in with a couple of Spaniards this afternoon," Hob said, and told Harry about Lawyer Molinez and Architect Fernandez.

Harry Hamm was the former policeman from Jersey City, New Jersey, who had come to Ibiza for a vacation and married the beautiful Maria. He had been cozened by Hob into enlivening his retirement by working for the Alternative Detective Agency.

Hob had started the Alternative Detective Agency because he wanted a job without regular hours that would make enough to keep him in Europe. Private detectiving seemed ideal for a person low on skills but with a good deal of luck and a lot of friends. It gave him a chance to employ his friends, who, like him, were a tribe of homeless exiles without a country they considered their own and without allegiance to any but their own kind. Hob had a lot of friends. He had met most of them from among the uncountable thousands that poured in and out of Ibiza every year, and, like him, were seeking the Great Good Place and the Life That Worked. They were the disinherited and disenfranchised of the world, chaff of the technological revolution, meaningless data of the electronic age, superfluous people, and they didn't have to be black or Hispanic to fit into that category.

So Hob founded the Alternative Detective Agency as a sort of a floating commune centered in Ibiza and Paris, with excursions elsewhere as the spirit moved him or the opportunity presented itself. He staffed it with people like himself, wanderers and misfits, artists and would-be artists, visionaries with uncommercial visions, con guys who always got taken, tough guys who were forever getting beaten up. Hob had little expertise, but his rates were low. He wasn't tough, but he had a dogged quality. His intelligence was only average, but he scored high on whimsy. The Alternative Detective Agency didn't prosper, but it kept him and several other people alive, and gave him something to do on the long nights when he wondered what he was doing on this alien earth.

Harry was large and overweight and solid, with close-cropped white hair. "That doesn't sound good," he said. "Do you think Don Esteban is up to something?"

"Not a chance," Hob said. "That old guy is the soul of honor."

"People change after an illness," Harry said.

"What illness are you talking about?"

"Esteban had a stroke while you were away in Paris. Didn't you know?"

"Nobody told me," Hob said. He had been back in Ibiza now for less than a week. He saw he had a lot of catching up to do.

"I used to see him all the time," Harry said. "But since the stroke, he doesn't come out anymore. Have you called on him recently?"

"No. I've just got back."

"It might be a good idea."

2

The next day Hob visited Esteban's farm. Esteban's wife, Amparo, was as unfriendly as usual. She had never liked Hob. She said that Esteban was not well and was not seeing any visitors. Hob had to be content with that. He went back home, thinking deeply. Although he was still sure nothing was wrong, he was starting to get worried.

He ran into Don Esteban a day after that, in Luis's store. Esteban had aged visibly. His hair had turned white. His hands shook. He nodded vaguely at Hob. His sons bundled him into the family SEAT, the Spanish version of the Fiat, and got him away before Hob had a chance to exchange more than a few words with him. The old man's voice had begun to quaver, and his sparse hair had begun to drop out, balding him and leaving him looking uncomfortably like a newborn babe, or perhaps even more uncomfortably, a freshly skinned rabbit.

Hob was beginning to worry. He ate that evening at La Duchesa restaurant, presided over by Liana, the small, redheaded French Basque lady who had married Moti Lal, the well-known Parsi Indian painter who spent most of the year in Paris but summered in Ibiza.

Liana said, "Eh, Hob, good you came in. Harry wanted to see you. He's eating in the back room."

One of the charms of Ibiza in those days was the lack of telephones in private houses. Phone service at this time only extended to commercial establishments and government offices. People had to leave word for their friends in bars and restaurants, or trust in luck, or, in a final extremity, drive out to their houses, if they knew where to find them in the web of dirt roads that connected the tangle of steep hills that formed Ibiza's backbone.

Harry was enjoying a plate of pork chops in brown sauce to which Liana had given a fanciful Catalan name. Hob sat down and ordered the roast leg of lamb.

"I looked into this matter of Don Esteban and your finca," Harry said. "Asked a few questions. Paco at the San Carlos store filled me in on most of it."

Hob already knew that Esteban's sons needed money and had been driven crazier than they were already by the old man's conservative ways. Hob also knew that Ibiza, after many years of neglect under the Franco government, had put in a jetport and was experiencing a boom. People on all sides were making land deals and selling formerly worthless property for fortunes. Every year, Ibizan property went up in value. Hob knew all that. But he hadn't considered how much the brothers feared prices would fall as suddenly as they had risen, leaving them holding half a dozen worthless farms that the old man out of sheer stubbornness had not sold even though he didn't work them or rent them out. The farms just sat there, a wasted asset, and wasting an asset was unthinkable in a frugal peasant economy like Ibiza's.

The rest of the properties would come to them after Don Esteban's death. But this one place, C'an Poeta, was in the twilight zone, owing to the discrepancies between the written and the oral agreements concerning it. Hob knew this, too.

What was new to him was the fact that C'an Poeta was of considerable interest right now because a Madrid syndicate wanted to turn the house and its surroundings into a tourist hotel, gambling club, and disco.

Don Esteban had turned them down. Then he had his stroke.

Amparo and his sons browbeat him into showing them a copy of the *traspaso.* They read the contract and found that there was a large final payment due on July 15 of that year. It was the sort of payment easily promised, easily overlooked. In the old days, Don Esteban would never have enforced it. But it was the sort of clause that Lawyer Matutes had insisted on putting in. Interpreted in strict accordance with the law, it meant that if he missed the payment Hob could lose the property.

Hob thanked Harry, finished his dinner, and went back to his finca. The next morning he went to the Los Almendros Café in San Carlos, where they had the telephone closest to him. After some difficulty he was connected with the telephone in the back room of the Bar Balear in Ibiza City. Hob's lawyer, Don Enrique Guasch, along with most of the other lawyers of the island, made this his headquarters, for here one could order wine and coñac and nibble tapas all day and grow as fat as a Catalan lawyer ought to be, and stay in close contact with his friends and enemies, the other lawyers and the judges.

After suitable greetings were exchanged to the desired degree of elaboration needed to denote the close relationship between the two men, Guasch got down to business and told Hob he had been about to send a messenger to find him. He had bad news.

"Let me have it," Hob said. "It's about the house, isn't it?"

"I'm afraid so," Guasch said. He then regretfully told the middle-aged American private detective that he owed a million pesetas on the lease on C'an Poeta and that it was due July 15 and that they, the Esteban family, were notifying him as required in the contract, so that he would have fair warning that upon his inability to pay the required sum, the property under discussion, C'an Poeta, situated in the parish of San Carlos on the north shore of the island, would return to them, the original owners, Don Esteban and the people speaking in his name.

This hadn't been Hob's understanding of the arrangement at all. He drove directly to Don Esteban's farm in San Lorenzo to get it straight. Amparo, Don Esteban's unfriendly wife, again wouldn't let Hob in to see Don Esteban. She put him aside with evasions. "The old man isn't well today. He's staying in his room. He doesn't want to see anybody. If you want to leave a message, I'll make sure he gets it."

Peering in, Hob saw the two sons, Juanito and Xavier, lounging in soft chairs in the *entrada*, grinning at him.

Hob drove straight into Ibiza City and found his lawyer, Don Enrique, still in the back room of the Balear, playing dominoes with an old crony. He allowed Hob to take him across the promenade, to the Cellar Catalan, for a second lunch and a private conference.

An hour and a half later, Hob went back to his finca a sadder and wiser man. The Estebans had him over a barrel. He was going to have to come up with the money. Luckily, a million pesetas at that time was only about ten thousand dollars, and ten thousand dollars, though a very respectable sum, was not by any means the end of the world.

Unfortunately, Hob didn't have that relatively insignificant sum. He had just about nothing. And there was an additional complication: Mylar.

Mylar had been Hob's wife at the time he signed the *traspaso*. Hob had put Mylar's name on the contract in a moment of good feeling. He and Mylar had gone down to Hob's lawyer, Enrique Guasch, in the port of Ibiza. It seemed that something was not correct in form, and the *traspaso* had to be made over again. It was just a matter of getting some dates straight. Guasch had shown him where to sign.

"Right here. *Propietario.* And *propietaria*, if it applies."

Hob had hesitated. He'd had no idea before this that he was going to put Mylar's name on the document. She had nothing to do with the finca, which he'd acquired long before he met her. But she was looking very pretty that morning, and it was a brilliant, sparkling Ibiza day when just being alive makes you feel immortal, and they had been getting along well for several days. Hob was in love that day, had been for several weeks. A record for him.

After that, of course, the disillusion set in. Mylar had a strangeness about her that was charming, even intriguing, before you got to know her better. After that, it was just maddening. Their good time had been in the off-season, before the summer sun and the carnival atmosphere of the island drove Mylar, who was still called Janie then, a little crazy, or crazier than usual. This was just before her affair with Rebecca, the ersatz baroness from Holland, when Mylar was just starting to discover her lesbian identity and disillusioning poor straight old Hob, who wasn't with it at all and was still stuck in the old one-man one-woman bag.

But all that was to come later. For that moment, standing in the lawyer Guasch's office, it was Ibiza and youth forever, you and me against the world, babe, and hell yes, darlin', put your signature right there, we'll be co-owners of a bit of paradise.

And now it was some years later and Guasch was telling him all this over a second lunch in the Cellar Catalan. Guasch was fat, round, jolly, wised-up, with an ailing wife and an alcoholic Swedish girlfriend who ran a souvenir shop in the port.

Guasch had confirmed Hob's suspicions. "No, Don Esteban didn't fiddle with the *traspaso.* I doubt he even glanced at it before signing it. That sort of balloon payment at the end came in with the Romans. I wouldn't say it's illegal, but it's awkward for you. You should have let me strike out the balloon payment clause before you signed it. Of course, you didn't know me very well then and you did know Don Esteban. Or thought you did. See, here, they've demanded the million-peseta payment immediately when due, on July fifteenth of this year. Or you forfeit your property."

"I've lived there for five years," Hob said. "I've made a lot of improvements. Can they really do that?"

"I'm very much afraid they can. They're within their rights. You have one month, less a few days. But what's a million pesetas to an American, eh? Excuse me, I make a poor joke. I know your circumstances. You have exactly twenty-seven days to get your money together, pay it, get your title clear. It comes to just under ten thousand dollars. Have you got it?"

Hob shook his head.

"Can you borrow it?"

"I doubt it," Hob said. "Unless . . ."

"I'm so sorry," Guasch said cheerfully. "Do you think you can get it?"

"I'm going to get it," Hob said, with more confidence than he felt.

"Try to get it before the next devaluation, no telling if you'll win or lose by that. And I regret to emphasize that there's no way of staving this off. Staving, is that the correct word? Unless you could get Don Esteban to change his mind. And I doubt you'll have much success at that. He's gone quite senile since his stroke, you know, and has become the creature of his wife, the deadly Amparo, you should have known *her* mother, and that skinny priest from San Juan, and the two boys. You know they want to sell to the Sport Club, don't you? They're offering them one hell of a lot of money. You had the bad luck to choose a finca with the prettiest view on the island. Too bad you can't sell the view and keep the rest. Get the money, Hob, and be sure to get Mylar's quitclaim, that's also essential."

Hob went home to his finca. He didn't speak to anyone, not even the Rafferty twins from Los Angeles who were friends of Hob's sister and who were clipping the grapevines, not even Amanda, Moti's fashion model girlfriend from Paris who was making curry in the kitchen. He went straight to his room. His own, private room, as distinct from the rest of the finca, where up to a dozen friends and friends of friends stayed from time to time. His room was a bare, whitewashed cube with a small balcony. The view was spectacular. Opening the French doors you could look out through a cleft in the distant mountains and see a narrow blue window of the sea, framed in almond blossoms provided by the tree that grew just outside his window. Hob looked at the view critically and tried to convince himself that it was too pretty for real beauty, but without success. He liked it just as it was. His eye knew every fold of land, every tree and hummock on his property, every *algorobo* in his fields, every almond tree in the side orchard. Well, he was going to have to raise that ten thousand and get that quitclaim.

Unfortunately, this came at a low point in his finances. He'd never had many high points. But this was an especially bad time. The Alternative Detective Agency wasn't earning much money. In fact, it was losing. Hob had to put out for taxes, bribes, stationery, and folding currency with which to pay his operatives. This all added up to a net loss at the end of this year, and not much better the year before.

At least he could do something about Mylar. She'd been after him to return to America and give her a Jewish divorce. It seemed that Sheldon, her tax accountant husband-to-be, had Orthodox Jewish parents who insisted upon an Orthodox Jewish divorce before they'd give their approval. And their money, though no one mentioned that part, went hand in pocket with their approval.

At the time she asked him for it, Hob had resisted. They already had a legal divorce, what did they need with another? Additionally, Hob hadn't wanted to return to New Jersey and New York. For one thing, it cost money. For another, bad things happened to him in the metropolitan area. He had a sense that it was a bad idea to leave the island at this time. But he was forced.

Even raising the plane fare was not easy. He managed it, though, calling in petty debts from all his friends and getting a three-hundred-dollar loan from the wealthy English actor who lived nearby and had been none too pleased at being thus tapped, but made the loan anyway.

And then he booked his trip on Iberia, wiring Mylar to expect him and set up the divorce, and said farewell to the island and his home. He had the curious feeling that Ibiza was leaving him, not the other way around.

3

THE FLIGHT WAS uneventful. Upon arriving at Kennedy, Hob went to the Iberia Airline counter to check the personal messages, just in case Harry Hamm had come up with any late-breaking news on the *traspaso* situation. There were no messages for him.

That done, Hob took a bus to Snuff's Landing, New Jersey. He had to change in Jersey City to make the connection. It took him almost five hours to get from Kennedy to Main Street, Snuff's Landing.

Snuff's Landing was an unprepossessing little town on the western shore of the Hudson River, sandwiched between dank Hoboken and dreary West New York. Hob had made it with less than ten minutes to spare, and so he went directly to the rabbi's house on West Main Street, which was about three blocks from where Hob used to have an office and close to the Snuff's Landing house on Spruce, which he was signing over to Mylar in exchange for clear title to C'an Poeta.

When he arrived at the rabbi's house, the rabbi's wife ushered him into a parlor smelling of shoe polish and potato latkes, where Mylar was waiting. His ex-wife was tall and good-looking, and wearing a dark, severely cut business suit and a necklace of Polynesian shark's teeth over a cotton Mickey Mouse T-shirt. Mylar's fashion statements had always tended toward the oxymoronic. Ex-husband and ex-wife shook hands in a formal manner, but with smiles to show that they really didn't mean anything bad by this. It was time for amused little jokes, banalities such as "I see divorced life agrees with you," since it had been six months since the actual civil divorce. But Hob couldn't think of any witticisms, funny how they can fail you just when you need them most, and Mylar was not being forthcoming. She felt in an awkward situation, because this Jewish divorce had been forced on her by Sheldon's mother, who had insisted on it before she would allow him to marry Mylar. All Hob could think to say was, "Well, two years of marriage down the tubes," and he decided to suppress the remark. Instead he pulled the transfer-of-ownership document that Guasch had given him, and offered it to Mylar with his pen, remarking, "Might as well get this over with."

Mylar gave him a certain look, but she had agreed to this in return for Hob flying back to New Jersey and giving her this divorce. And he was giving her the Spruce Street place, though its value had been reduced considerably since the fire. She uncapped the pen, gritted her teeth, and was about to sign away her share of the Ibiza dream when the rabbi's wife came into the room and said, "The rabbi is ready for you now." "I'll do this later," Mylar said, and handed the pen and document back to Hob. They followed the rabbi's wife into the study.

In the rabbi's study waiting for them were two small, bearded men with big black hats, and a large man wearing a yarmulke. The large one with the embroidered yarmulke from Israel was the rabbi, the skinnier of the two remaining was the scribe, and the remaining man, who had a mole low on his left cheek, was the witness.

When Hob came in, the scribe picked up a varnished mahogany case in which, resting on crushed velvet, was a quill pen, a penknife with a mother- or perhaps niece-of-pearl handle, and a hollowed-out cow's foot filled with ink. He handed the tray and contents to Hob.

"What's this for?" Hob asked.

"He gives it to you as a gift," the rabbi's wife said. "You see, you're supposed to bring your own pen and ink and parchment, like in the old days, but nobody does that anymore. Who knows from quill pens nowadays except a professional scribe? And so he gives them to you so they'll be yours, so you can loan them to him so he can write the *get,* the parchment of divorce. And when it's all over you make him a present of his pens and inks back again."

"Suppose I want to keep the pen?" Hob said.

"Don't act silly," the rabbi's wife said. "Here, put on a yarmulke. Go ahead. They're waiting."

"Draconian," the rabbi said to Hob. "Is that a Jewish name?"

"We got it at Ellis Island," Hob said. "My grandfather got it, I mean."

"What was the original family name?"

"Drakonivitski."

"But why did he change it to Draconian?"

"In our family," Hob said, "we think Grandfather must have met an Armenian immigration official who couldn't resist the temptation. That's only a theory, of course."

The rabbi shrugged. The fee was paid, and if these people wanted to act like meshuggeners, that was their business.

"And you are Rebecca Fishkovitz?" he said to Mylar.

"I changed it," Mylar said. "My name is Mylar."

"First or last?"

"Both. Or neither." She smiled, having succeeded once again in spreading confusion.

"Mylar is a kind of plastic, is it not?" the rabbi asked.

"A very pretty plastic," said Mylar with her bright smile.

The rabbi had had enough small talk. He got down to business. He asked Hob if he really wanted to divorce this woman. Hob said he did. But, the rabbi said, is there not some chance that, given time, you might change your mind? Impossible, Hob said. The rabbi asked a third time, and a third time Hob declined. Then came the part where Mylar had to walk around him three times. She floated around with her usual grace. Hob noted that she looked more radiant on her divorce than she had on her wedding. Sign of the times, he supposed. Then there was the return of the silver, the ancient bride-price, here represented by five shiny quarters, which Mylar accepted with a smirk. And at last those words that bring happiness to as many as do the words of marriage: I divorce thee, I divorce thee, I divorce thee, said by Hob and repeated three times. And then the rabbi proclaimed them unmarried people according to Jewish law, and gave them the get, which he ripped almost in half in accordance with the usual practice.

They left the rabbi's house together and walked down West Main Street to where Sheldon was waiting for Mylar in his Ford Wrangler. Hob didn't want to talk to Sheldon just then so he said good-bye to Mylar at the corner. Then he remembered the *traspaso.*

"Oh, the *traspaso,*" Hob said, handing it and his pen back to Mylar. Mylar took it, uncapped the pen, then hesitated.

She said, "We really don't need this formality. I know the property is yours. You had it before you met me. You don't think I'd do anything against you on this, do you?"

"Of course not," Hob said. "But you know how Spanish courts are. The formality."

"I guess so," Mylar said. She scribbled her signature and handed the pen and document back to Hob.

"Take care of yourself, Hob."

"You too, Mylar."

She turned to go, then stopped. "Oh, by the way. Max Rosen telephoned you."

"Max Rosen? Who's he?"

"He said you'd remember the sea urchins on Sa Comestilla Beach."

"Oh. Okay. What did he want?"

"He wants you to call him. I've got his number here somewhere."

Mylar rummaged through her purse and found a Kleenex on which a New York telephone number had been written in blurry lavender lipstick. She handed it to Hob.

"Good-bye, Hob. Thanks for the divorce."

"Good-bye, Mylar. Thanks for the *traspaso.*"

She gave him a cheery little smile and walked off to Sheldon's Ford Wrangler, parked up the street. Hob watched her go, and within him there wasn't even a sigh.

Still . . . two years of marriage down the drain.

4

Hob left Mylar at the corner of State and Main and walked to his former office on State and Third. He had occupied one room in a dentist's suite. It had been a few years since he'd paid any rent, but the place was still unrented to anyone else. The sign over the door read, Draconian, Private Investigator. Everything Our Specialty. Discretion Assured. He climbed a flight of stairs, went down the hall past the dentist's office on the left—Goldfarb, Orthodontic Surgeon, the Overbite King—to a pebbled glass door at the end. On the outside it said, Draconian. P.I. Hob fitted in his key and opened it.

Gray autumnal light came in from the windows facing State Street and the Hudson River. At the end of a short corridor, he came to a single smallish room with a battered oak desk and a typing chair. Another chair, an armchair, was positioned just to the left of the desk, and there was a straight-backed chair to the right. On the left wall was a four-drawer filing cabinet. On one wall, which was painted a faded green, hung a copy of somebody's painting of Minnehaha, Daughter of Laughing Waters. Oddly enough, there was no story attached to this painting. Hob couldn't remember how he had acquired it. He suspected it was Mylar's touch, put in when he hadn't been expecting it. There was also an ancient Smith Corona portable typewriter on a gray felt pad. That also had no significance, in fact even less than the painting.

Hob sat down behind his desk. He wished he had a felt hat to scale at the coatrack in one corner. The coatrack was another of Mylar's touches. He felt somewhere on the line between nothing and crappy. Divorcing Mylar for the second time had none of the exhilaration of the first time. It was time he got back to Europe, even though he had just gotten here.

But there was work to be done. He needed to find some money. That, he reminded himself, was why he had come back to the States. The thing with Mylar was just a sideshow. But where was he to get some money?

Sea urchins. Yes, he remembered. On the beach at Sa Comestilla.

Max had been a houseguest of Carlo Lucci, a retired textile man from Milan. Lucci had put Max up in the guest cottage on their estate, Son Lluch, just outside the old lead mine, not far from San Carlos. Hob met him at El Caballo Negro, the "in" bar in Santa Eulalia. All this was before Mylar's time, of course, when Hob was still living with Kate and the kids. Nigel Wheaton was off the island that summer, off on some harebrained scheme in Belize. With Nigel away, it was a quiet summer. Max Rosen, then working in New York as a theatrical agent, had come to Ibiza for a holiday, had rented a boat locally from Texas Tom Jordan, and had invited a bunch of people for a day on the waters; Hob had been included. It was a thirty-foot catamaran that Texas Tom had built himself, then gone off to Kathmandu and never returned. Hob had a lot of time on his hands that summer. He ended up spending some of it with Max on the catamaran.

One time they'd anchored off the beach at Sa Comestilla. Max had brought along a prepared lunch from Juanito's restaurant, not Juanito Esteban, Juanito Alverez from Barcelona. Cold roast chicken, potato salad, green salad. Max had remarked that what was needed was a nice appetizer.

"You want an appetizer?" Hob asked him.

"Sure. But so what?"

"Hold lunch for ten minutes. I'll bring you an appetizer."

Max stood up, a hefty figure in white jacket and slacks bought at Hombre on boutique row in the port of Ibiza. He looked around. They were anchored fifty feet off the beach.

"Where are you going to get this appetizer?" one of the girls asked.

"Don't worry your pretty head over it," Hob told her. He was already in swim trunks. He fit a face mask over his head. Didn't bother with the fins. The water was no more than ten feet deep. He did remember to take along a mesh shopping bag, and a pair of canvas gloves. Then he was over the side and kicking down to the bottom.

The water was clear, and the sandy bottom was gleaming white. Scattered along the bottom were some black things about the size of saucers. As Hob came down to them he could see their spines. He carefully lifted half a dozen of them and put them into the shopping bag. Then kicked for the surface and swam back to the catamaran.

"What's this?" Max asked.

"Sea urchin. Delicacy of the Med. What we need now is knives, forks, and some lemon."

"What's it like?" one of the girls, the one with the long brown hair, asked.

"Raw sea urchin is not to everyone's taste. Don't ask me to describe it. It tastes a little like crab and a little like caviar."

Max liked it, and the girls raised no objections. Ibiza girls eat anything.

Afterward, Max relaxed on the deck under a brandy-soaked Mediterranean sun. "Hob," he said, "this is wonderful. All of it. Ibiza. The sea. The sky. The land."

Ahead of them, the island of Ibiza rose out of the flat, shining sea. It was a perfect day in July.

Max said, "This is the best summer of my life. If you're ever in New York . . ."

Hob made the call to the New York number Mylar had given him.

5

The woman's voice over the telephone was clear, low pitched, well modulated.

"Max Rosen Associates."

"I'd like to speak to Mr. Rosen."

"Who shall I say is calling?"

"Tell Max it's the guy who taught him how to eat raw sea urchins near the beach at Sa Comestilla."

"How do you spell that?"

"Which part?"

"That last word. Com something."

Hob spelled it for her. She still didn't like it. But she was a good sport. "Just one minute." She switched him over to the Muzak. It was playing something with a lot of violins while outside his office window, a couple of kids were playing stickball.

Suddenly there was a man on the line. Deep booming voice filled with vitality.

"Is this who I think it is?"

"Yes, it's Hob Draconian."

"Hob! What a pleasure! You got my message. What are you doing in the States, anyhow?"

"I came back to take care of some business."

"How's the detective business?"

"Going great, Max."

"No, seriously."

"A little slow."

"Can I help?"

"Only if you're fool enough to invest in an unlicensed American detective who has an unpaid *traspaso* on a beautiful finca in Ibiza."

"I might be able to help. What's the deal?"

"Max, it's a straightforward proposition. Invest with me and I go spend it on my *traspaso.* I've got a problem there. You get your return off the top if I ever show a profit."

Max thought it over for a moment or two, turned it over in his mind, tasted it and found it good. "Listen, maybe I can help. What the hell, you're practically family. Where you calling from?"

"Snuff's Landing, New Jersey."

"Well, come on into Manhattan. I've got plenty of room here. You'll stay with me. We'll get shit-faced and talk about the old days. You're here for the weekend? I'll show you a time you'll never forget. What was that girl's name in Formentera? Never mind, we'll talk about it when you get here. How are you coming?"

"Trailways bus."

"You don't have to do that, Hob. Take a taxi. I'll leave money at the desk."

"I'm not too proud to ride the bus."

"I am. But suit yourself. I'll have Kelly meet you at the Trailways in Port Authority."

"Hey, that's not necessary. Just give me the address." But Max had rung off. Hob wondered who the hell was Kelly.

6

While Hob was walking to the bus stop, Lieutenant George Glatz was rubbing his forefingers together. It was the sort of meaningless gesture that had begun to plague him more and more of late. He leaned back in the seat of the paint-sick Pontiac that the Third District police headquarters on Dulcimer between Tenth and Jade had assigned him. "Perfect for surveillance," Captain Kirkpatrick had told him when Glatz had asked for the Corvette. "A car like this, one look and you can't remember what it looks like."

Glatz was parked in the special zone that the airport people assign to police officers who have to shadow someone leaving Kennedy. In this instance, Glatz was supposed to follow a man named Santos, a diplomat from the newly independent Caribbean state of San Isidro. Since Santos was accredited to the UN, Glatz couldn't arrest him even if he did something. So why was Glatz there? Why was the NYPD interested in Santos in the first place? Because certain persons from Treasury, so it was rumored around the big water cooler that stood next to the bulletin board just down the hall from the sergeant's office in New York's Third District police headquarters, had had a short but intense talk with Commissioner Flynn at Flynn's castle in Rhinebeck, New York, and the result, after clanking its way down the chain of causes and effects for a few days, was to put Glatz in a paint-sick Pontiac in the special police no parking zone at the international arrivals building of Kennedy International Airport.

Glatz was not alone. Sitting in the passenger seat beside him was a DEA agent named Emilio Vasari. He was presently working undercover on a case that involved Santos, at least marginally.

Glatz sucked on a Chesterfield filter. He was tall and cadaverous, with close-cropped brown hair beginning to thin and gray, and a long nose with a bump in it from the time he had played center-field tackle for the Gaelic Striders and had briefly contemplated going on the professional hurling circuit until a batsman's boggle not only broke his nose but also damaged his optic nerve so that it was almost a year before he could see the same old crap with his previous acuity.

His car telephone rang.

"Lieutenant Glatz? This is Angelo at customs."

"Yeah, okay, what's up?"

"That guy you were asking about—Santos—he's just coming through now. Want us to give him a toss?"

"Certainly not," Glatz said. "He's got diplomatic immunity. Just pass him through. Thanks, Angelo."

Glatz put down the phone. Turning to Emilio, he said, "He's here. Maybe we'll get lucky this time."

"Huh," said Emilio. He had some problems of his own to think about.

The Varig jet had begun its flight in Rio de Janeiro and made various stops in the Caribbean and at Miami before it landed at Kennedy Airport. The passengers came forth, first class first—money has its privileges. There were only five passengers in first class. Four of them had that anonymous gray-suited bebriefcased and gold-watched look that could enable them to pose anywhere as a frieze for Wealth and Its Privileges. The fifth man, Santos, was something else again, though not too much of a something else. He was a tiny man who wore a little pointed beard and looked like a miniature Robert De Niro. Santos's face was a matte brown, his eyes were clear with the tiny wrinkles in the corners that you get from dodging palace revolutions. He wore diplomat's blue pinstripe. In his lapel there was a tiny rainbow-colored pin: the Order of Simón Bolívar, awarded to him by the government of Venezuela in recognition of his service there as ambassador from the island of San Isidro. His shoes, perhaps not surprisingly, were patent leather pumps with elastic sides. He carried himself erectly. There was an air of alertness to his face. An ironic smile shaded his lips; the expression seemed habitual.

Santos strolled through the resounding corridors of Kennedy with the other passengers, toward immigration and customs. He had a little mustache as well as the beard, an imperial, it was called, and he looked like one of those third world diplomats who are more at home in Manhattan than in Misraki, San Isidro's capital city and main port. At the immigration desk he took out a diplomatic passport and showed it to the official. The slight pursing of the official's lips would have presaged no good for one who was not, as Santos was, a diplomat fully accredited to go where he wished and do what he wished in the United States without let or hindrance. His baggage and person were not to be searched under any circumstances, even suspicious ones. The customs man, seeing that this man was untouchable, and in any event pursuant to previous orders from Glatz outside in the paint-sick Pontiac, unpursed his lips, stamped Santos's passport, and watched him go through the green doorway of nothing to declare, from which place, unchallenged to open his sturdy attaché case, he continued to the baggage claim and ground transportation.

The official picked up the phone on his desk and punched in a three-digit number. He heard a terse, "Yeah?" and said, "Your guy's just left."

Down in the short-term parking lot Glatz put down his car telephone and snubbed out the cigarette that Alice had said only that morning was going to kill him, the only question was when, and the sooner the better as far as she was concerned. Alice had been in a bad mood ever since they cut back on her methadone, telling her that eight years of maintenance was enough already. Glatz sighed. He supposed he'd gotten what he deserved. His dad had always told him, never marry a junkie, not even a Catholic junkie.

"He's coming through now," Emilio said, and Glatz cranked up the paint-sick old Pontiac and a moment of expectation hung in the warm summer air.

7

When Santos came through the automatic doors onto the passenger pickup area, Jose, the embassy driver, was just gliding to the curb in the big old stretch Cadillac. Jose was the best driver San Isidro had ever produced. The stretch limousine pulled in just as the ambassador came out the swinging doors. Santos always considered that trick of Jose's more difficult than balancing the island's budget. Not that anyone tried very hard to do that. Santos got in, taking care not to step on Paco, who was lying on the floor of the car under a throw rug.

"Good trip, sir?" Jose asked from the front seat.

"Yes, tolerable," Santos said. "Always good to go back home, as long as it is not for too long. How are things here?"

"The usual soap opera," Jose said. "Undersecretary Juarez is making a fool of himself again with the daughter of the ambassador from the Dominican Republic—do you know, there's no short way of saying that?—and as usual his wife is the last to know. Secretary Shirley Tschombola is pregnant, we believe by Gardener Felius. And there have been a few other incidents."

"Pretty much business as usual," Santos said. "Good, good." Then he remembered the man lying under the throw rug at his feet. "Paco, how are you?"

"Welcome back, sir," Paco said in a muffled but respectful voice.

"Don't get up yet," Santos said. "Not until we're out of the airport area. Nobody saw you get in the car, did they?"

"No sir. They smuggled me in at the embassy garage and I've been under this rug ever since."

"Good, good. We'll talk later."

They went around the ramps and onto the Belt Parkway that led to Manhattan. Jose had already determined that an old Pontiac was following them. Soon the cemeteries of Queens came up on their left, and beyond them, the highly taxed skyline of New York City.

"Okay, Paco," Santos said. "We can talk now. But don't sit up."

Paco pushed aside the throw rug revealing himself as a short, chesty, weight-lifting sort of vaguely Indo-Latino sort of a guy, with sideburns that came to scimitar points just above the muscled and knotty line of his jaw.

"Did you bring it?" Paco asked.

"Of course" Santos said. "The plan must go forward."

Paco nodded. He was five and a half feet tall by three and a half feet across the shoulders. He came from Matelosa Province, San Isidro's poorest district. Paco's family had worked for two hundred years on the Santos family estate. There existed between them a master-slave relationship that both men cherished.

"I think you ought to know," Jose said from the front seat. "We're being followed."

"That's all right," Santos said. "I counted on the possibility. Paco, let's get to work."

Santos opened his diplomatic pouch. Pushing aside a small sheaf of state secrets that was there only as window dressing, he took out a small canvas bag that looked like it weighed about two kilos and might have a street value of perhaps two hundred thousand dollars, assuming the bag contained two kilos of 99.9 percent pure cocaine from the family estates of Santos's cousin Octaviano Marrani from Cochibamba Province in Bolivia.

"You know what to do?" Santos asked.

"I know," Paco said. "Don't worry, boss."

"Easy for you to say," Santos said. "The outcome of a multi-million-dollar dope operation isn't your responsibility, is it?"

"I know it's not easy for you," Paco said.

"And why do I bother doing it? After all, I am independently wealthy."

"You do it for San Isidro," said Paco. "For your *patria,* and mine."

"Yes," Santos said. *"La Patria."* He smiled bitterly. "Is it not strange to what extremities the emotion of patriotism can lead us? To think that we would be doing this!"

Jose the driver leaned around from the front seat. His mustache quivered as he said, "Those people are still following us."

"I hadn't expected them to go away," Santos said. "Can you lose them?"

"Here in the Midtown Tunnel?"

"Sorry, I forgot. When possible."

They came out the tunnel into Manhattan. The Pontiac was about four cars back. All of them watched the pursuing car in the rearview mirror and pretended to an unconcern they could not have felt. When they came across town to Seventh Avenue, Jose picked his moment and made a quick right turn that took them momentarily out of sight of the pursuing vehicle; then Paco opened the door and slipped out into the street. He had the satchel clutched tight.

"Now take me to Godfrey's," Santos said, after Paco was gone.

The limo turned and would have sped away if this story had been taking place in California. Since it was New York, the limo crawled crosstown and then uptown again, and, eight cars behind it, Lieutenant Glatz struggled along. Unnoticed by either car, Paco had picked up a new pursuer. Another car, a brown Ford Fairlane with a crumpled right front fender, had been following the Pontiac all the way from Kennedy. The two men in it had a better angle and saw Paco leave Santos's car. They spoke to their driver and he stopped. They got out and followed Paco on foot.

8

THE RIDE ON the Trailways bus to the New York Port Authority building was interesting in a dreary sort of way. Hob sat beside an elderly man in a greasy green parka who told him all about a car he had only had for seven hours before his ex–son-in-law totaled it. Hob tuned out the old guy's babble, mentally reviewed the list of people he was going to call for a loan as soon as he was in Max's apartment, and watched through the window as the bus negotiated the spirals down to the Lincoln Tunnel. He started thinking about Mylar. She'd looked really pretty this morning at the lawyer's office. He remembered the sweet look on her face the morning just a little more than two and a half years ago when he'd married her at the British consulate in Gibraltar.

The Trailways bus came through the Lincoln Tunnel and parked in the bay under the Port Authority bus station. As Hob got off he saw a short, heavyset, middle-aged man with a tough, expressionless face watching the passengers get off. He was holding up a sign that read Hob Draconian.

Hob went up to him and said, "I'm Hob Draconian."

The man reversed the sign. On the other side it read Welcome to New York.

"I'm Kelly," the man said. "Max sent me out to get ya."

Kelly was solid and compact. He was wearing a starched short-sleeved cotton sport shirt with small horses printed on a white background, olive drab slacks, plain brown shoes well shined. He had a pale, closely shaven face with a strong five o'clock shadow. A smell of lilac toilet water emanated from him. Hob remembered that you could still find lilac water in the old barbershops of the financial district and Little Italy. Kelly had a diamond pinkie ring and small brown bloodshot eyes. His voice was husky New York, friendly but impersonal. He looked like a man you don't fool around with. Not that Hob was planning to.

Kelly led him to the escalator. They went up to street level and went out on the Ninth Avenue side. There was a shiny new Chrysler stretch limo parked in a No Parking zone. A cop was standing beside it, rocking back and forth on his heels and twirling his nightstick. Kelly said, "Thanks, Dugan. I appreciate it."

"Any time, Kelly," the cop said.

Kelly opened the limo's back door for Hob, remarking, "I used to be a cop myself. Sergeant. Homicide."

They drove uptown to one of those big new apartment buildings near Lincoln Center. There was a man in uniform to open the door, another man at the front desk.

"Who did you wish to visit, sir?" the deskman asked Hob.

Kelly said, "This is Hob Draconian, Max Rosen's friend. He'll be staying for a while."

The deskman said, "Mr. Rosen didn't say nothin' ta me about it."

"So call him up and ask him yaself."

The deskman considered, shrugged. "If you say it's okay, Kelly."

Kelly lead Hob to the elevators, muttering, "Them fuckin' Greeks."

Hob didn't make much of that. He watched as the floor numbers flashed by. They blurred into one another and he lost count after about fifty. It seemed a long time until they reached the penthouse.

He followed Kelly down a carpeted corridor to a door marked Penthouse. As if you couldn't tell. Kelly took out a key and let them in.

9

Hob found himself in a big bright white-walled room with shiny parquet flooring. At the far end, a picture window looked out over Manhattan to the south. There was a spindly antique-looking desk near the door, and a woman with brown hair in a pageboy sitting at it was talking on the telephone. She was about twenty-six years old, with a broad, attractive face. She was wearing a brown tweed sports jacket, and a straight black skirt that showed off her crossed legs to advantage. Beneath the jacket she had on a pale peach blouse. Metal loop earrings. A string of small pearls.

She said into the phone, "Look, I'll get back to you," and hung up. She turned to Hob and Kelly.

"Hi, Kelly." She gave Hob a bright smile. "You're Hob?"

"I am."

"I'm Dorrie. Max'll be right out. Can I get you a drink?"

"Thanks, no."

"Max will dispense the other refreshments himself. Take a seat, you're home."

Hob found a leather couch near her desk. The ten-foot wall behind it was bookcases to the ceiling. Each bookcase had eight shelves and each of those shelves was packed, crammed, and jammed with movie cassettes. There were more cassettes on the end tables, and even a few on the floor in the tiny kitchen area.

Back in Ibiza, Max had mentioned that he liked movies. There was a Sony super beta and a Panasonic AG 6810 VCR, and beside them a Sony thirty-inch television. The other walls were covered with photographs of models, signed and framed. There were several Fashion Institute awards on the walls of the corridor. There was soft snarly rock music playing on a music system. There were smells of marijuana and freshly roasted coffee.

That was all Hob had time to observe because just then Max came bounding into the room. He was a big man, a little heavier than Hob remembered him. He was wearing a gray Italian silk business suit with a red tweed tie. On his feet were unpolished Scotch-grain brogues. He had a large florid face framed in wavy black hair that was just starting to gray. His handshake was firm, and he put his other hand on Hob's shoulder and squeezed. His large brown eyes were moist, shiny.

"Hob! Goddamn but it's good to see you! You've met Dorrie? This office couldn't run without her. Hob, that summer in Ibiza was the best of my life."

"It was a good year for me, too," Hob said.

Max grabbed Hob by both shoulders and shook him playfully. "You know, I was always planning to come back to Ibiza."

"But you never made it."

"I was afraid I might stay for good."

"You're kidding."

"Maybe not. I'm getting rich, Hob, but I don't have much fun." He made it sound pathetic.

"At least you've got plenty of movies."

Max glanced at the bookcase full of cassettes and grinned. "Yes, and plenty of dope, and plenty of just about everything else except . . ."

His eyes slid away. "This is gloomy talk. Let's lighten up, huh? Have you eaten? We've got a place here does the finest spareribs you'll come across this side of Greenville, North Carolina. And I suppose you wouldn't mind a toot?" He took a two-gram glass vial out of his pocket and handed it to Hob, along with a gold-plated single-edged Pal razor blade. "You can cut it on the glass tabletop," he said.

"Not just now," Hob said.

"Don't be bashful, just tie into it. This stuff is Blue Killer from Bolivia." Max uncapped the bottle and poured out a pile of crystalline white powder with a bluish glitter. It looked like some of that Mother Crystal the druggies were always talking about when they discussed dream shipments that never came through.

"And a snorter, of course," Max said, handing Hob a gold-plated straw flared at one end.

"Max," Hob said, "I'm not using it anymore."

Max stared. "You've got to be kidding. Hob? Old Hob the Demon Drugger? Going religious on us? Come on, babe, loosen up!"

Hob shrugged, smiled, and accepted the snorter. He'd taken no hard drugs at all for over six months. His doctor in Paris had convinced him they weren't much good for his atherosclerotic arterial system. His own good sense, what little of it that was left, told him that he paid for every high with a long dark low.

But it was hard to refuse. Dorrie was watching, eyes bright and cynical. And you know how it is with old dopers. Hob's fingers took the snorter and set it into the ready position. Max opened a desk drawer and handed him a six-inch slab of onyx with two long fat wavering lines of white powder running from one end to the other. Hob's nose began watering in anticipation as he bent over and snorted up his first line. That first hit was immaculate. It was like talking to a long-lost old friend. The stuff exploded in his sinuses. His pleasure circuits lit up. A giggle of laughter bubbled up inside him. A voice that he wished weren't his own said to him, "Just this once, it's going to be all right."

Cocaine is an unusual substance, but the idea of it being a master drug is laughable. For most people it's a one-time high. After that you habituate fast, and it does nothing for you but increase your already strong susceptibility to self-deception. But it would be too dismal to face up to the fact that after one fine party, all your great highs are in the past, along with your good intentions. This time Hob got a slight flush, about what you'd expect from from the first cigarette of the day. And with it there came the bad taste in the back of his throat, the irritability, the jagged nervousness that always accompanies cocaine. He took a second line to get over the effects of the first, to get into the good part, the high, and then a third line because the second didn't quite get him off. As usual, the self-deception was kicking in nicely.

That broke the tension, if there had even been any. Max took a long double snort and then Kelly took a snort, drifted to a couch and picked up a newspaper, high but on duty. Dorrie took a small snort and then answered the telephone. And Hob, once started, kept at it doggedly as Max kept on pouring more high-priced powder onto the onyx.

Hob's good intentions went out the window before he had even gotten a chance to form them. Maybe it was because of Mylar, because, although he was glad the marriage was over, the world seemed a less optimistic place without her. And maybe he was taking it because he'd suddenly had the thought that a weekend with Max, whom he'd only known for one summer more than ten years ago, might not have been such a great idea. And he was upset about the *traspaso* and the whole Ibiza situation. How could Don Esteban have done this to him? He almost dreaded returning to Ibiza, and yet he knew he had to get back as quickly as he could and stave off what looked like the imminent loss of C'an Poeta and perhaps a whole way of life. Despite the coke, or maybe because of it, he was getting nervous, depressed. He wasn't even going to get time to get over his jet lag. He knew he just had to hold himself together until his sense of purpose returned. Meanwhile balm of Gilead, hair of the dog, he poised the snorter and sucked in long wavy lines of Blue Killer or whatever they were calling the stuff this season.

Phones rang and Max had to get back to work in his interior

office. "Kelly'll show you your room. Later, babe." Max went inside. But Hob didn't leave the living room at once. He was busy doing coke, and Kelly was matching him line for line and talking about some sport, basketball maybe, Hob wasn't sure.

Over the next hour Hob took enough Bolivian marching powder to run a locomotive to Albany and back. And didn't feel a thing. Not at first. And when he did feel something, it was fatigue.

They call it paradoxical effect. All dopers know it. It is when the drug does the reverse of what the people around you say it's supposed to do. Like finding yourself unable to sleep because you're tanked up with sleeping pills. Or unable to stay awake because the coke or the amphetamine has hit you wrong.

At some point Max came out of the back office. Hob did a few lines with him, and remembered saying, "I need to make some calls. Then I think I'd like to lie down."

"Good idea," Max said. "I should have warned you about this stuff. Bet you never get this quality in Europe. Come on, I'll show you your room."

He led Hob to the back of the apartment. There was a second suite of rooms back there—small living room, adjoining bedroom and bathroom.

In a corner of the room there was a glass coffee table covered with drugs: little bottles of cocaine, plastic baggies filled with marijuana, bottles of different kinds of pills. There was the inevitable large flat onyx stone with a pile of white powder on it, a gold razor blade, a gold snorter. There was also a crystal decanter on the table filled with a clear liquid, possibly water, and a couple of wineglasses.

Max introduced him to the pills. "This here is Ritalin, in case you need to smooth out, and this here's Percodan. These little green ones with the hole in them are a Mexican variety of Valium, and this one here I can't remember its name but it's a Brazilian form of Quaaludin."

Dorrie called from the other room, "Long distance, Max."

"Enjoy," said Max, and left.

Alone in the suite, Hob unpacked his suitcase, humming to himself, suddenly feeling very good. He hung up his clothes in the closet, pausing to take another hit or two of the coke. Then he sat down on a couch. Suddenly he was not feeling so good.

Nevertheless, he took another line, a big one, and started making calls on the Mickey Mouse telephone beside the day-bed.

Half an hour later he had called everyone he could think of in the New York area. Most of them had been out. Those who had been in had not been sympathetic. I'd love to help you, Hob, but this is a crazy time. . . . Five calls, not one cent raised. The *traspaso* fell due on July 15. Today was June 19.

Kelly knocked and came into Hob's room.

"I gotta take Max over to Shreiber's, he's late for an appointment. He'll be back as soon as he can. He says make yourself at home. You okay?"

"Oh yeah," Hob said.

"You feeling okay?"

"A slight indisposition," Hob said.

"I think you're not used to this shit," Kelly said, indicating the coke. "Here, take one of these, fix you right up."

He shook a little gold-speckled purple pill out of a bottle, handed it to Hob, and poured him a glass of water from the decanter.

Old habits die hard. Hob swallowed it without thinking. Then asked, "What did you give me?"

"Just one of them muscle relaxants. A Korean formula. Catch you later, kid."

Kelly left.

Hob wondered if he should have taken the pill. In a few moments a smile crossed his face. He was feeling no pain. He pulled off his sneakers and lay down on the bed. There was a stereo within easy reach. He turned it on. Peaceful music flooded the room.

He settled back, closed his eyes, time for a little nap.

10

WE'RE LOOKING AT a beautiful old house made of weathered stone, rectangular, with graceful lines based on the golden mean. A classic Mediterranean look. A grape arbor just inside the courtyard. Beyond the house we can see a thin edge of the blue Mediterranean. It is early morning. There is a chill in the air.

The open double doors, both very high and wide, lead into a gloomy interior. It is a room with a brownish concrete floor and a high-beamed thatched ceiling. It is the living room of Hob's finca, the one he lived in before C'an Poeta. To one side is a faded but expensive-looking Persian carpet. There is a low stuffed couch against the wall. It is covered in clashing soft paisleys. Two cats are sleeping on the couch. Next to it there is a large low oval table made of hammered brass. A three-foot hookah sits on the table, beside a plastic ashtray stamped Brown's Hotel, London. There are three gaily colored and uncomfortable-looking beanbag chairs slumped around the table like gut-shot hoodlums in red velvet suits. The room is illuminated by two Aladdin kerosene lamps in simulated brass, with white glass shades with tiny blue cornflowers on them.

To the left there is a staircase leading up to French doors. Beyond them is Hob's office. Within, Hob sits at an unpainted plywood desk in front of a big Olympia manual typewriter. There are sheets of paper in unkempt piles on the table's surface. Hob is typing furiously.

There is a voice from downstairs. It is Kate, just coming out of the kitchen, twenty-two years old and very pretty, blond hair streaming down her back, looking like the spirit of the flower generation.

"Dinner's ready!"

Hob: "I'll be right there. Just have to finish my wordage."

Kate: "How many pages today?"

Hob: "Twelve. I'm just finishing."

He ducks back inside, returns to his typing. We follow and look over his shoulder. He is writing, "Now is the time for all good men to come to the aid of Hob Draconian." Over and over. And we see that the other pages contain the same message.

The scene blurs, fades out, fades back in, changed. It is that wonder of wonders, a snowy morning in Ibiza. The finca gleams white against the lightly powdered ground. The almond and carob trees are stark silhouettes against the pale sky. It is all very unreal. Hob and Kate put the last suitcases in the car, an inexpensive Citroën Dyane 6. The grape arbor is withered now, the cats nowhere to be seen. The car, parked in the lane outside the garden wall, is so loaded with luggage that it sags on its axles.

Hob goes inside and closes the big front doors, then locks them with a cast-iron key weighing at least a pound. Hob and Kate get into the car and drive off, down the rocky driveway and onto the blacktop road. The hillsides of Ibiza stand on either side, the beautiful biblical scenery, low hills, sheep and goats, orchards, rocky land, low stone walls, stone farmhouses. They drive a mile, then turn off to a dirt road. They go to a farmhouse, get out of the car. A couple, Spanish peasants by the look of their clothes, come out to meet them. Hob returns the key. The farmer goes inside, brings out glasses on a plastic tray, a bottle. The farmer pours two small glasses of *hierbas.* Everyone drinks to everyone else's health. Everyone hugs everyone else. Hob and Kate go back to the car. The Spanish couple start crying as they drive off. When Hob and Kate see that, they can't stop from crying, either. They drive off slowly toward the port of Ibiza.

Kate says, "That's that."

Hob says, "We can work it out."

Kate says, "Oh, Hob. I want to so very much."

Hob says, "But what about Nigel?"

"I'll just have to tell him that it's all over between us. But do you mean it this time, Hob? Are you really through running away?"

"I'll never leave you again," Hob tells her.

Now suddenly we cut back to the earlier scene, the big white finca on the steep hill above the main road to Figueral. The camera lifts and pans the Morna Valley, then continues panning and we see, just below the shimmering blue line of the sea, the white edge of the beach at Aqua Blanca.

Unaccountably, it's spring. Kate is wearing a dress made up of light-colored gauzy layers that float in the breeze. She smiles. Her honey-colored hair frames her face. The tiny spring flowers are in bloom—little irises and dwarf orchids, and bright red poppies. The sky is very blue, and there are a few fragile clouds very high up, close to heaven. Hob and Kate stand close together, looking at each other. This is it, the culmination, the realization of the impossible dream.

Then a man's voice says, "Excuse me, sir."

11

PACO DUCKED OUT of the car, stuffing the canvas bag that Santos had given him under his shirt. It was a guayabera shirt, pleated in front, and the package stretched out the pleats somewhat. Not that Paco cared. Although he was a careful dresser when life gave him the opportunity, he was not fussy. He had been accustomed to good clothes for only a few years, since Don Santos had brought him up from the family hacienda in Matelosa Province on the eastern side of San Isidro, and installed him in the New York embassy.

He walked uptown on Seventh, crossed over to Eighth, reached Forty-first Street and went into the Port Authority building. His senses were super alert. He was prepared for this moment, had been ready for a long time. His was a small part, but a vital one. And he was aware that he was a vital link in the revitalization of the San Isidrean economy. Yes, he and the people he worked with, Santos and the others back home, were the one last bright hope of the San Isidrean people, their only chance of taking their rightful place under the bright sun of human progress.

His professor of ecocatastrophes at the University of San Isidro, a man they listened to respectfully, though behind his back they called him Humberto D, had first opened his mind to the peril run by third world countries just by the ineluctable nature of things. "Don't let America and Russia fool you," Humberto

D had thundered from his lecture stand in the main lecture hall of San Isidro's university. "Their ideological battle is camouflage. It covers up what the real fighting's about: namely, who's got the money and how to keep it from everyone else. It's a poker game, my friends, and the smaller nations are going to be tapped out. At Harvard this is called the poker table theory of economics. The third world is going to default and United Fruit and its ilk are going to inherit the pot. The best we can hope for is some nice international company to build a convention site here and give our people employment as waiters. The trend is set unless we reverse it ourselves." Here he held up his crippled hand and smiled bitterly. "It is up to you, young men and women of the nation, to give little San Isidro a chance."

There was never enough money. But education was the first priority. The planners at the Financeria had figured that beginning from a base of a few hundred million, they could turn the University of San Isidro into a first-rate education facility, and from that all else would flow. Since San Isidro's population was small, it would allow every adult San Isidrean to retire from his other pursuits for a period of three years, paid for by the government, in which time he would be taught the fundamentals of modern history, science, literature, art, geopolitics, mathematics, ancient languages, and so on.

"In the future," the professor said, "the choices will be simple. Either you will design chips or you will assemble them. If you can't be the brains, you'll be the hands."

How was San Isidro to become the brains? By training. And how was the training to be paid for?

As the American folk hero Clint Eastwood says, Any Which Way You Can.

One avenue of national growth became quickly apparent. San Isidro was conveniently located for the dope trade. It was a small island in the Caribbean 170 miles from Barranquilla. It had a major airport because of its large cut-rate cruise business. Another money-earning outlet would do no harm, and now was the perfect time for it. The heat was tightening up around the Colombian supply. Some important people had flown in from Medellín to consult with Dr. Sachs-Alvarez, the president. The upshot of it was, Dr. Sachs was offered a 10 percent cut on gross shipments and was allowed to introduce his own line, San Isidro Pale Bash, which it was hoped would soon be much in demand among discriminating drug users.

To choose international crime hadn't been easy for Sachs, a Lutheran minister who had started life in Stockhausen working on the docks, and had come to San Isidro almost thirty years previously by a route that involved a long stay in Shanghai and a longer one in American Samoa. In the end, Sachs had succumbed to the lure of improving the lot of his poor undernourished pellagra-stricken people who contested with Haiti for the lowest position on the world poverty charts.

San Isidro had nothing. San Isidro had lost its trees ages ago, its mineral-poor soil had been used up both for farming and for mining. Its waters were fished out. Nobody wanted to start a semiconductor plant in its festering suburbs. The World Bank loaned it 20 million or so a couple years ago as a Christmas present, but there were other, more promising candidates now. And anyway, the money had all gone into vaccine to fight the plague the UN inspectors had brought—Norwegian White and Blue Fever it was called, a disease that caused the infected to die babbling of fjords. By the time it was settled, the San Isidreans were no better off than before. What was there left to do but turn to crime? Happy the country that had even that possibility, no matter how morally indefensible.

President Sachs had turned the execution of the problem over to his right-hand man and UN representative, Olivier Santos y Manchega. Santos had brought up the all-important first shipment, the first sample of the Mojo, the White Babbler, the San Isidrean Giggle Dust, the Pale Bash. It wasn't much trouble getting it into the country. That part was safe enough. Even if they suspected you, they didn't open diplomatic pouches, that would spoil it for all their friends. It was the next parts that were going to be difficult. Because selling San Isidrean coke involved a lot more than finding a market. There was the international cartel to think about, and they were more dangerous than the feds. Although he had the cooperation of the Medellín cartel, the boys from Cali had different ideas. Still, Sachs thought he could get things going.

"Remember two things," Sachs had told Santos before he left.

"What's that?"

"Don't let the feds get you. And don't get ripped off."

Unfortunately, there had been no time to fix the police and DEA people at New York. Santos had been annoyed about that, but it couldn't be helped; arrangements were made for longtime players, new boys in the game had to take their chances. It was a delicate situation. Santos understood that the New York police liked corruption, and also liked rigorous efficiency. It was always hard to tell which you were going to get.

New York being a weird place made it all the worse, of course.

New York itself was but a transshipment point. The new place for drug expansion was Europe.

And so Santos had turned over the sample bag to Paco, his loyal family retainer. Paco would handle the next step.

Paco was thinking about all this, as a man will as he strolls up Broadway with a couple of kilos' worth of product in a canvas bag snug against his brown belly with the faint line of black hairs up the middle, and not paying too much attention to what was going on around him, since it seemed to be nothing more than New York up to its old tricks again, the usual city scene, the typical stick. Or so it seemed.

A moment later, Paco had changed his mind. His wide-set eyes, with their visual periphery extended far beyond that of an ordinary civilized man, a bit of his Caribe Indian heritage, picked up subcues he hadn't even been consciously searching for. His attention was caught by a movement curiously out of synch with the movements of others, there on the extreme threshold of the farthest edge of his seeing. Paco left the Port

Authority, went uptown, turned at Forty-seventh Street, glancing into a store window as he turned, and saw, in the darkly reflecting glass, two men who by the suspicious auras they gave off, as well as a certain reptilian alertness to their close-set eyes, seemed to be following him.

12

Hob opened his eyes. Standing near him, a look of concern on his mild face, was a middle-aged, light-skinned black man wearing neatly pressed jeans and a blue work shirt. He was balding; iron gray tufts of hair encircled his ears. He wore steel-framed glasses. Around his neck on a thin gold chain was a small gold Star of David.

Hob sat up. Apparently he had fallen asleep in his clothes. Sunlight was streaming in the window, so he couldn't have been asleep too long. His nose felt and smelled like a rotted Idaho potato. His sinuses ached from having been a battlefield for crystalline substances decaying in his mucous membranes. He had a dull headache at the back of his skull; it was the sort of ache that can't be distinguished from incipient brain tumor. Aside from that, he was fine.

"Who are you?" Hob asked.

"I'm Henry."

"Do I know you?"

"I don't believe so. I'm Henry Smith, Mr. Rosen's cleaning man."

"Hello, Henry. I'm Hob Draconian. I'm a friend of Mr. Rosen's."

"Yes sir. I figured you was a friend."

"Is Mr. Rosen still out?"

Henry looked puzzled. "He wasn't here when I got here."

"When do you expect him back?"

"I don't expect him at all. He just leaves my check on the fridge. I come every Saturday. Sometimes he's here, sometimes not."

Saturday. That was curious. Hob had come to Max's on Friday. Henry must have gotten his days wrong.

"I think this is Friday, Henry."

"No, sir. This is Saturday."

"How can you be sure?"

"Because just before I come here I go to shul every Saturday at the Ethiopian Israelite Synagogue on a Hundred Thirty-seventh Street and Lenox Avenue."

Hob pondered. His brain felt ever so slightly paralyzed. He was having difficulty making sense out of the simplest propositions. At least, he assumed they were simple. So this was Saturday. That meant he'd been out cold for about twenty-four hours.

Well, he'd been tired. Jewish divorces really take it out of a guy. But the real reason, of course, was the combination of cocaine and that gold-speckled purple pill, the blockbuster muscle relaxant that Kelly had given him. If the brain is a muscle, that stuff really worked.

"You look kinda unsteady," Henry said, watching Hob get to his feet. Hob felt like a newborn deer taking its first steps. He looked like a gut-shot giraffe. Henry reached out and steadied him before he tripped over a wall. "Kin I git you some coffee before I go?" he asked.

Hob almost refused: Hell, that's all right, I can get it myself, just point me toward the kitchen and give me a little push. But then two thoughts crossed the deteriorating tabula rasa of his mind. The first was, I'd give almost anything to have a cup of coffee brought to me and put into my shaking hands. The second was, once Henry was out of the room he could take a couple of lines and pull himself together.

"Thanks, Henry, if it's not too much trouble I'd appreciate coffee very much."

Henry went into the kitchenette and quickly made Hob a cup of instant coffee, using the hot-water tap. He waited until Hob sipped it, then said, "You okay now?"

"I'm fine, Henry," Hob said. "Did Mr. Rosen say when he'd be back?"

Henry shook his head. "He never tells me nothin'. I just clean up. Anything else you need?"

Hob shook his head.

"Then I'll be gettin' along. See you next Saturday, if you're still here."

As soon as Henry left, Hob opened the drawer on the coffee table and found the big onyx stone. Henry had put it away neatly. The coke was still on it, as were the blade and the snorter. Henry must be really reliable, cleaning up stuff like this every Saturday and not getting whacked out of his head. Or maybe he was religious.

If this was Saturday . . .

Hob had to face it, if the guy had just been to shul, this was Saturday.

So where had Friday gone? For that matter, what day had he left Ibiza? Something was out of sorts, him or the time. He decided not to think about it just now. He'd lost a day. What would he lose next? He cut two small lines and snorted them. The cocaine burned. His sinuses winced in response. Then his head cleared. The delicious numbness of incipient peritonitis invaded his gums. He felt a whole lot better: there's nothing like cocaine to alleviate the condition it creates. For the moment he resisted the temptation to take another couple of lines. The telephone started to ring.

Hob decided to ignore it. But it's difficult to just let a telephone ring, even if it isn't yours. Ringing telephones demand to be answered. Still, Max must have his own system for dealing with phone calls when he was out. Maybe he just didn't bother with them, figuring, if it's important, they'll call back.

The phone continued insisting. After another twenty or so rings, it stopped.

Hob finished the coffee. He opened his suitcase and unpacked his meager wardrobe—an extra pair of jeans, a few shirts, a change of underwear, and a heavy Formentera sweater in case there was a cold snap in July. He went to the guest bathroom and took a shower. That helped. He shaved, and that helped even more. Then he dressed and went out into the living room.

The Betamax and the VCR both looked terribly complicated with their little red and green lights and all those switches and dials. It wouldn't do to break his host's toys. He decided to look them over later. Meanwhile he was hungry. He was about to go check out the kitchenette when the telephone started again, and then another telephone somewhere else in the apartment joined in. Hob didn't answer either of them. He decided to check out the apartment, just in case Max was lying dead or unconscious somewhere.

In Max's bedroom suite, on the other side of the living room from where he was staying, Hob came across an open bureau drawer. Inside it were several sets of keys. Underneath the keys he saw more little bottles of coke and pills. But no grass, which he could really have used. Below the bottles, held together with a thick blue elastic band, was about fifteen hundred dollars in hundreds. Under that was a blue steel Smith & Wesson .38-caliber revolver. Hob didn't touch either. Sometimes those things have hair triggers. As far as he could tell, it was loaded.

He was looking at the gun, the drugs, and the bills, and thinking night thoughts, when he heard the phone begin again. At the same moment, there was the sound of a key turning in the front door lock.

13

IT TOOK THREE keys to open Max's front door. Hob listened while the locks clicked one by one. Then the door opened and in walked Dorrie, Max's assistant, whom he had met earlier—twenty-four hours earlier, if Henry was to be believed; and if you can't believe a black Jewish cleanup man who doesn't steal his boss's coke, who can you believe? Dorrie was wearing tweed trousers and a black turtleneck.

She said, "Do you know how long it takes to get here from Brooklyn Heights?"

"Half hour?" Hob hazarded.

"Try an hour and twenty minutes including a fifteen-minute delay under the river."

"I'm sorry to hear it, but that's hardly my fault."

"Of course it's your fault," Dorrie said. "Max has been trying to call you for hours, but where you come from they apparently don't answer telephones. Or maybe you weren't sure what that ringing noise was."

"We've heard of them in Ibiza," Hob said, "but we don't trust them."

"That's obvious. Anyhow, Max phoned me and asked me to come up here and find out if you were alive or dead, and, if alive, to ask you to pick up the goddamn phone, he wants to talk to you."

She glared at Hob, beautiful and aggrieved, and just like that

Hob was in sticky and familiar territory, accused of not performing a deed he had thought better left undone. He had hardly met Dorrie and already they were sounding like the terminal stage of a marriage on the skids. Hob reminded himself never to marry her; heavy dating would be plenty.

"Why are you looking at me with that weird look?" she asked. "Isn't my makeup on straight?"

"You know, you're beautiful when you're mad," Hob said.

She stared at him. Her sails were all set aback by the head wind of his oxymoron. It was obvious to him that she was a nut for ambiguity. He noticed that her lower lip glistened.

"You're quite crazy," she said at last.

"I'm not, you know. It's just my complicated way of asking you out to dinner."

Hob could see her trying it on for size. Something was going on between them. Or at least between him. His heart was pounding. Cocaine kickback or genuine human emotion? Or is there any difference?

The telephone, long threatened, rang pat upon the moment. Dorrie and Hob looked at each other and at the telephone. The telephone looked back at them with its silly beige face with the numbers on it. It rang and rang, pleading, raging—they're so childish, these telephones. Hob was determined to wait it out. Me Tarzan, you Telephone. But Dorrie lost her nerve and answered it.

"Yeah," she said, "he's here, your old Ibiza buddy." She handed Hob the telephone. "It's for you. I'm going to make some coffee." She walked out into the kitchenette.

"Max?" Hob said.

"How ya doing, babe?" Max said.

"What's up?"

"Hob, I got a favor to ask you."

His voice, despite the energy he put into it, sounded thin and far away.

"Where are you calling from?"

"Paris."

"Paris, France?"

"I sure as hell don't mean Paris, Texas."

Hob called out to Dorrie, "He's in Paris."

"I know," Dorrie said. "Cream and sugar?"

"Black."

Max said, "I beg your pardon?"

"Max, are you really in Paris, France?"

"Hob, so help me God, I'm in Paris, France. I'm in the Hotel du Cygne on the corner of Montparnasse and Raspail."

"But how could you be in Paris?"

"Big old jet airolino, baby. Get's you there in like nothing flat."

"All right," Hob said, "you're in Paris. So what else is new?"

"That's better! Look, Hob, a business matter came up suddenly. I had to get over here quick to close a deal. I'm going into partnership here with the Dartois Agency. This is big, babe, very big. In about a week I'm going to be a part owner of the biggest model agency in Europe *or* America. And that, my boy, is not piffle."

"Congratulations, Max."

"Thanks. Reason I called, I need one of my models over here soonest. Her name's Aurora. Aurora Sanchez. I don't suppose she's called in while you were there?"

"No, sorry," said Hob.

"Well, I need her here. I promised her to Montmorency to headline his new spring line. She's going to be his model of the year. It'll make her one of the world's top models, and it'll close my deal with Dartois."

"That's great, Max."

"Yeah, I know. But I got to get her here. Hob, I want to hire you to find her and put her on a plane to Paris soonest. You go with her. I want you to hand-deliver her to me. This is important, Hob. Will you do it?"

"I guess so," Hob said. "But two days isn't much time. How do I get the tickets? Has she got a passport? And where do I find her? And by the way, what are you paying me for this?"

"I knew I could count on you," Max said. "There's ten thousand dollars in this for you, Hob. What you need, baby. Can't say fairer than that, can I? But you have to drop everything else and get right on this."

"For ten thousand dollars," Hob said, "I'll wipe my appointment calendar clear for the next week. Hell, I'll give you two weeks."

"I just need two days, Hob. But you have to bring her to Paris. As for the tickets, I've already reserved them in your name. You can pick them up at the Air France office at Kennedy. There's a flight in the morning leaves at seven A.M. You've got to be there an hour early. Your passport is in order?"

"Don't worry about my passport. What about Aurora's?"

"I made sure she had one when I was still in New York. I've been hoping to put this deal across."

"Okay, now where do I find her?"

"Got a pencil and paper? Okay, here are some addresses and telephone numbers." Max talked, and when he was finished, Hob read the names and numbers back. "That ought to do it. There's a little leather-bound address book on the desk in my bedroom. Dorrie's number is there, and Kelly's. You'll find walking-around money in the left-hand drawer of my bedroom bureau. Also plenty of you know what, in case you need it. My number here at the hotel is in my address book, too. This is where I always stay when I'm in Paris. Just do this for me, Hob. Get Aurora and get her here."

"She's not going to balk, is she?" Hob asked. "I charge extra for drugging people before I put them on an international flight."

"Are you crazy? When she hears about this, she'll kill to get to Paris. You're not going to have any trouble with this one, Hob. Just do it! Okay, babe?"

When Hob put down the telephone, his hands were shaking. Another little line? No! He had work to do. This was the finest break of fortune he'd ever had. This little job could set up the agency properly, pay the *traspaso,* and with what was left over from the fifteen hundred dollars walking-around money he could get something to Harry Hamm in Ibiza, and something to Nigel Wheaton wherever he was, and to Jean-Claude. All he had to do was find a girl named Aurora and get her to Paris. How difficult could that be?

14

Dorrie, all business, opened her big purse and took out a folder. "Here's the information I have on Aurora. You'll note she lives on East Sixty-sixth Street near East River Drive, directly crosstown from here. Here's the number of the photo studio where she does most of her work. We have the number and address of an aunt in Brooklyn, but she's never there. Also the number of the church she goes to, also in Brooklyn. Here are some photographs of her. That's it. Is there anything else I can do for you before I go home?"

"You tell me," Hob said. "Is she due to be going out of town for any reason?"

"Not that I know of." Dorrie looked at her watch. "It's almost two in the afternoon. You've got the rest of the day and all night to find her. Your flight to Paris leaves at seven A.M. from the international departure lounge at Kennedy. Kelly will take you. He ought to be here now—"

She stopped, hearing a key in the door. They waited. The door opened and in walked Kelly.

"Kelly," Dorrie said, "I don't know if you know about the Paris thing—"

"I know," Kelly said. "Max phoned me at the gym. I came right over." He looked at Hob. "You and Aurora gotta take the morning plane from Kennedy, right? Meanwhile, I'll take you wherever you need to go. I've got the limo downstairs. I'm ready to go any time you are. You got much luggage?"

"Just the one suitcase," Hob said. "It's in the bedroom. I just have to throw my stuff back in it."

"Don't bother, I'll do it for you. I'll put it in the limo for you."

"I still have to find Aurora," Hob said.

"You shouldn't have any trouble. She's usually home if she's not on a shoot or out with Max."

"I'm about to find out," Hob said. "So if you'll excuse me, I've got a call to make."

"I'm leaving," Dorrie said.

"I'm going into the kitchen and get a beer," Kelly said. "Do you know if Henry brought up any? Never mind, I'll find out for myself."

Kelly left the room, and Hob could hear the hard heels of his footsteps as he walked to the kitchen. Dorrie picked up her purse, gave a jaunty little wave, and left the apartment, closing the front door firmly behind her. Hob settled down to the telephone.

He dialed Aurora's number. The line was busy.

15

"HELLO, AURORA? THIS is Max."

"Damn it, Max, you stood me up last night. Where are you?"

"You're not going to believe this, baby."

"Try me."

"I'm in Paris."

A pause at the other end. Then, "You're kidding, aren't you?"

"Baby, I'm serious. I'm at the Hotel du Cygne just off boulevard Raspail. You remember the place, don't you?"

Taking a deep breath. Forcing herself to remain calm. "What are you doing there? I thought the next time in Paris was going to be you and me."

"That's what I'm setting up. Listen, babe, you remember that little matter I was talking to you about? That little matter of Dartois making you model of the year?"

"Yes, Max, I remember you saying that very well."

"Well, something just came up and I think I can swing it now."

"Max, how wonderful! When should I come over?"

"In the morning. I've got it all set up. Someone is going with you. But it's not quite as simple as that."

"I should have known there'd be problems."

"Well, to swing this thing with Dartois, as you'll remember, I need money."

"Max, you got money."

"Not the kind I need to buy into Dartois. I need about two hundred thou more."

"This was the way it was yesterday, Max. I don't see what has changed."

"What has changed is, I've got a way to get up the money. You remember that other matter I was telling you about? It's on. And I've had a visit from a friend I told you about. Hob Draconian. He'll be calling you soon."

"What about?"

"I've told him to find you and bring you to Paris."

"I still don't get what you're up to, Max."

"He's a private detective. I'm paying him to do this."

"But why?"

"Listen, babe, do I have to spell it out? Santos called from the airport. He just arrived. He's got the stuff for me. Paco is going to give it to you."

"Max, you live in New York, the world's prime drug market, and you want to ship the stuff out to Paris?"

"Yes, I do. It's a business deal. The New York market is already sewed up. I don't have the contacts to sell it in a single piece in New York. And I won't be there to sell it off in eighths like I used to. With this stuff here, I can swing the deal with Dartois, which'll get you model of the year and give me what I want."

"Max, if you think I'm going to carry that stuff over, you're crazy. I told you I got problems with Emilio."

"You'll just have to duck him."

"And bring that stuff through customs? You tryin' to get me a jail sentence?"

"Darling, believe me, the fix is in."

"So why don't you carry it yourself?"

"Because I'm in Paris, not New York."

"I won't do it and that's that."

"I've got a way to do it without risk. Like I said, you'll be accompanied by Hob Draconian."

"Yeah, so?"

"I'll tell Kelly to put the stuff in his luggage. It'll go right through."

"And if it doesn't, what about Hob?"

"He'll be all right, too. If they catch him, he'll convince them he didn't know anything about it, they'll hassle him for a while, but they'll let him go."

"You're sure of that?"

"It's more than likely."

"Hell of a way to treat a friend."

"Model of the year. And me a part owner of Dartois. Honey, the stakes are plenty big."

"Max, I don't like this."

"Aurora, please stop looking on the dark side of things. Nothing will go wrong."

"Okay, Max, he's your friend anyhow, not mine. So what shall I do, wait home for his call?"

"That's the idea. You'll go tomorrow morning. See you soon, babe."

16

Paco suddenly broke into a sprint. The men behind him ran after him. They were now above Rockefeller Center, Fiftieth Street or so, and Paco raced up, dodging pedestrians and bums, his footsteps, in their high-rise Keds, slapping softly against the dull gray pavement.

It was a beautiful day for a race through midtown Manhattan. Crowds just getting out of Radio City were treated to a flashing glimpse of these three men, running, the neckties of the two pursuers streaming over their shoulders, and Paco ahead, his big barrel chest pumping, dodging, running, turning, and all the time moving uptown, toward some unknown destination.

"Stop, goniff!" the foremost man behind him shouted. "I want to talk to you!"

"No speekee Eengleesh," Paco said, because you could never tell, a little indirection applied at the right moment could loosen up the frozen wheels of industry and render even the most dire of situations into a matter for merry laughing. Or so they had believed in his Swedenborg class at the university. Doggedly he shook his head. What nonsense a man could think while running! And he turned into Fifty-third Street. His legs stretched, pumped, bent, and straightened again, recapitulating all of the movements of a man running. Looking behind him, he saw his pursuers coming behind him, a pair of ugly men, one big, one small. Armed, no doubt. What lousy luck to pick them up just like that. He didn't dare go to his appointment now. He had to shake his pursuers. But how?

And then he was at a place with crowds in front, and he saw an opening and darted into the Museum of Modern Art.

17

Byron, the ticket seller at the Museum of Modern Art, really didn't want to let Paco into the museum because Paco looked like the sort of guy whose interest in paintings was limited to either stealing or defacing them. What would a guy like this with his big chest and his little beady black eyes be doing looking at paintings? And in those clothes!

It occurred to Byron to alert one of the guards, because this guy really looked like a wrong number. He began to reach for the security button but then he paused because Paco reminded him of somebody. He hesitated and tried to think who it is was, and then suddenly he had it: Goddamn, but the guy was a dead ringer for Diego Rivera! And Rivera was great, and much misunderstood!

So, although Byron wasn't quite sure what point he had made, he still desisted from sounding the alarm, especially since, just then, a tall, dark, handsome man came up, bought a ticket, and said, "It must be great to work here," and smiled.

Paco, meanwhile, walking on the first floor of the museum, was unaware of all this. Had they seen him go in here? Had they followed him in? His eyes darted back and forth like frightened black rabbits shrunk to the size of black-eyed peas. He looked outside briefly at the sculpture garden. It looked like a junk heap waiting to get filled in. He went back inside and made his way up the big marble stairs to the second floor. He waited for a while. No sign of the men. It was time for him to go out again and make the phone call.

The phone call. He had been dreading this part of it. Paco had a phobia about telephones. His father had died of an ear infection after pleading on the phone with a lieutenant from the tax office for a rebate on that year's tax due to bad luck and suicidal bad judgment. The old man had always had ideas like that. His illness had begun as a kind of fungus growth that formed a perfect circle around his ear. That was how he knew he had caught it from the earpiece of the telephone: the old and infected telephone of Paco's village, San Mateo de los Montes, in Matelosa Province, in San Isidro.

Paco had never revealed his telephonophobia to anyone. It had been too important for him to get this job. He wanted to come to the United States so that he could better himself. He knew that at some point he would have to do something important, that there would be something vital that he would have to overcome. The priestess herself, back when he had been an acolyte in the Church of Lesser Spirits, had told him, "There's no avoiding it, you know, a day of testing will come, a day when you will have to overcome what you've never mastered before."

"Can you give me a hint?" he had asked.

"You know that's not allowed," she said.

He had thought many thoughts since then, but it had never occurred to him, not directly, that is, though by unconscious routes, who knows?

Emerging from the museum, Paco walked down Fifty-third and saw a telephone booth. Yes, it happened as fast as that. In his pocket he found five quarters, which he had been playing with compulsively ever since leaving the embassy.

Taking a deep breath, he stepped into the phone booth.

Being new in these parts, he hadn't realized that the phone booth had a door and that that door could and perhaps should be closed. He dropped in a quarter.

After the coin dropped, Paco dialed the number that had been engraved in his memory through constant sessions with Santos, who insisted that he even learn it backward. The phone went through its usual repertoire of sounds. Paco had never before heard the sounds a phone makes, since he had never before talked or listened on a phone, owing to his phobia. But he had been farsighted enough to ask a friend of his, Ramon, a boy from his own village, to record for him on his own cassette player the sounds that a telephone makes, so that when the time came, when the hour of testing was at hand, he would not be helpless.

And it was miraculous to him that this telephone made the exact same sounds that Ramon's tape had revealed, though the sounds Paco was hearing were more sonorous, since this was after all the United States.

And then a tinny voice accompanied by static said, "Hi, this is Aurora Sanchez. I'm sorry I can't come to the phone just now . . ."

18

Nigel Wheaton, one of Hob's colleagues in the Alternative Detective Agency, was sitting bare-ass naked in an apartment in Paris reading a month-old *Times* of London. He was house-sitting Emily Schumacher's apartment while Emily was away in Provence on a painting holiday that included a special tour of Monet's garden and a stay at a quaint little local inn. It was a wonderful chance to combine painting with gourmet eating at a cost of only a few thousand dollars for the ten days. The tour guide was M. Grinette, the well-known expert on French impressionism. His wife, Mme Grinette, was the well-known columnist for *Haunch and Hoof,* the British gourmet magazine.

Emily could afford this trip because Emily was loaded. The tall gawky old widow had left Nigel in charge of feeding her cats and walking her dog, Quiffy. The dog was a suspicious chow who tolerated cats but didn't like people except for Nigel. Nigel had a gift with animals, a worthless sort of gift unless he wanted to become a veterinarian or open a pet store.

Nigel didn't. He hadn't been brought up to work at jobs like that. Not that he was lazy. Nigel loved to work on things, as long as they were pretty well guaranteed never to turn a profit. He did all the repair work and most of the rebuilding on his finca in San Jose, in Ibiza, before signing it over to his estranged wife, Nancy, in a fit of quixotic generosity. Nigel couldn't help acting rich even though he had no money. The Wheaton family had had a lot of money at one time. Enough to give Nigel and his brother Edward first-rate educations at Eton.

Edward, the sensible one, went into government. He worked in a nondescript government building in Bromley. No one knew just what he did. He was in one of the foreign sections. Something dull to do with trade treaties. Or at least that was the story.

Actually, Edward was in one of the spy sections, called by various innocuous-sounding initials, anywhere between MI5 and MI16. They changed the initials from time to time just to keep the opposition on their toes. This brother didn't actually leave his desk and go abroad a-spying. Cutouts, wetwork, field executives, these were all stuff of spy novels, which he never read. He left fieldwork to adventurous types like Nigel. Edward was content to stay in his office and push around papers.

That is not to imply that Nigel was in the Trade. It would have suited him well, of course, because Nigel was a swashbuckling adventurous sort of bloke who liked nothing better than to go hareing off to some place like Belize or Machu Picchu after hidden treasure. A James Bond type, but with an antipathy to government to which James gave only lip service. Nigel didn't like any government and therefore didn't care which party was in power. Despite this, Nigel did help out his brother from time to time when someone like Nigel was needed and no one with his talents but without his effrontery was available. But it didn't happen often.

The Wheatons had been rich, but something happened to the family money. Nigel went through his share of it during his gambling period. He had too much nerve to make a good gambler. To be successful at gambling you need to be frightened at the right times. And that house of his in Ibiza had cost a pretty penny, even with Nigel doing most of the work himself. And in the end he lost it all. Gave it away, actually, to his ex-wife, the beautiful Nancy, who, after all, had to raise the children.

So when all was said and done, there was Nigel, stony as an old boot, working for Hob and the Alternative Detective

Agency and waiting for something to turn up.

All that had turned up recently was this apartment-sitting gig in Paris for Emily Schumacher. It never occured to Emily, an old family friend, that she was *hiring* Nigel, like you'd hire some tradesperson. You don't *hire* friends of the family to sit your apartment and walk your dog. Perish forbid, as Emily was fond of saying, an expression she had picked up from her first husband, Barney, the bald and facetious real estate man from Albany, New York.

She'd run into Nigel walking past the Crillon one day, and asked him in for tea. "What are you doing in Paris, Nigel?"

"Just hanging around until the racetrack opens." Nigel would have died before admitting he didn't have the money to get anywhere else. You're really broke when you can't even leave town.

"Where are you staying?"

"I'm just between moves, actually," Nigel said vaguely. Actually, he was ashamed to admit he'd just been put out of an Arab rooming house in Belleville for lack of the old scratch.

"But how perfect!" Emily said. "You could stay in my apartment, then, couldn't you?" Emily explained that she wanted to go away for her ten days' painting holiday—she adored Monet but had never been able to copy him well—this was her chance to learn the trick of it—and she didn't have anyone to care for the animals. And she hadn't wanted to hire a service.

"They steal things. And you know how sensitive Quiffy is to strangers." Quiffy was the chow. "But she adores you."

Nigel had agreed. Emily had insisted on giving him money for the animals' food. Gave him her key, and was off that evening. Chortling. Husband safely dead, only son in Harvard, animals safe, and ten days with Monet and gourmet food. Who could ask for anything more?

Nigel was stony broke at the time. Any other man—well, most other men—would have taken the generous handful of francs Emily gave him and bought himself a square meal. Nigel went out and bought dog and cat food—tinned—best available—nothing too good for animals left in Nigel's care—and with what was left over, purchased two baguettes and a block of pâté. Not much of a planner was our Nigel. At the end of his third day in Emily's apartment, having consumed his provisions in a day and a half, Nigel raided the refrigerator and came up empty. Emily had cleaned it out some time ago. She ate all her meals out and didn't like to encourage spoilage. A search through the larder revealed nothing but two tins of cassoulet. Nigel consumed them on days three and four and was right back where he started from, only hungrier.

Nigel hated to think of practicalities, but an empty and growling stomach forced him to it. He looked around the apartment. There was plenty of bric-a-brac he could flog off at the flea market in Culaincourt. But he couldn't bring himself to do it. Suppose the hideous cut-glass decanter were missed? After all, this was a friend of his mother's! Hungry or not, he couldn't bring himself to steal from her, not even if he called it borrowing. Nigel was more capable of mugging someone on a back street in Montmartre than he was of imposing on the hospitality of a friend of the family.

Still, hunger gives its own advice. After phoning around to see if he could dredge up the odd franc from Jean-Claude—and finding him equally stony—and ascertaining that the other people he knew were out of Paris—probably playing the tables at Deauville and stuffing their faces at the lavish buffet—Nigel sat back on the sofa, lit a cigarette—he had seven Disque Bleus left—and eyed Quiffy the chow. Quiffy, not very bright even for a dog, waddled over to be petted.

"Quiffy, my dear," Nigel remarked, "you're putting on a bit of weight."

Quiffy, thinking she was being complimented, made a *kvelling* sound.

"Therefore," Nigel said, "you are going on a diet effective today."

Quiffy barked twice, sharply, signifying nothing.

"But so's you won't feel lonely," Nigel said, "I am going on the same diet with you. Half a can for you, half a can for me, of the best tinned dog food Paris has to offer."

And Nigel was as good as his word. He had long suspected that humans could survive in Paris indefinitely on the better brands of dog food. And if he was still hungry, he could steal a little kibble from the cats.

To make himself feel better, he reminded himself that he had eaten worse during that silly adventure in Ethiopia, and worse still in New Guinea, when he had accompanied Eric Lofton on his quest for the elusive bird of paradise, and ended up not even finding the guinea fowl of hell.

It was like Nigel not to complain of his lot, and not to do anything much about it. Stoical. Fatalistic. Except on points of honor. If it had been Jean-Claude, he would have flogged off the whole apartment, furniture and all, figuring that anyone who gave him this opportunity when he was hungry deserved what he got.

Nigel was reclining on the couch, naked in Emily's overheated Paris apartment, contemplating an ancient *Times* of London. A flash of red and gold—the goldfish turning in his tank. A squawk of yellow—the canary in his cage. Street sounds of Paris, but no accordion. Smell of burned coffee. Then the telephone on the polished mahogany end table rang in the lavish apartment on the rue Andre Breton just below the Sacre Coeur in Paris. Nigel made a long arm from the couch and picked it up.

He said in French, "Schumacher apartment, Nigel speaking."

"Nigel? It's Hob."

Nigel switched to English. "My dear fellow, how good to hear your voice. You're in New York, I presume?"

"Yes, but I'm leaving for Paris tomorrow morning. Flight three forty-two, Air France. Nigel, something very good has come up. I think I can pay off the *traspaso.*"

"That is very good news indeed," Nigel said. "I've been racking my tiny brain trying to think of some way to help out.

But at present I'm reduced to eating the kitten's kibble in Emily Schumacher's apartment whilst she leads *la vie bohemienne* in Juan-les-Pines."

"With a little luck, I'll be able to pay you something on account when I get back. Who knows? The Alternative Detective Agency may even show a profit this year. Listen, Nigel, have you got telephone privileges where you are?"

"Within reason, old boy, I can do what I please here short of selling the furniture."

"I want you to call Harry Hamm in Ibiza. I've been trying him but I can't get him in. Tell him I'm coming back to Ibiza with money for the *traspaso*, probably well before July fifteenth when it's due, God willing."

"I'll tell him. What is this sudden fortune you've come into?"

"Remember Max Rosen? The model agent?"

"Yes, I remember him."

"Well, he got hold of me here in New York. He needs a certain model in Paris tomorrow. Something to do with an important job for her. Model of the year stuff. He's paying me ten thousand dollars to bring her in. Plus a free ticket to Paris."

Nigel whistled softly under his breath. "Do you have to break her out of jail or something?"

"He wants her in Paris and he's willing to pay me to make sure she gets there. Ours is not to reason why. I'll see you day after tomorrow, Nigel. I'll be on Air France leaving New York tomorrow. You'll get right on this *traspaso* thing?"

"Count on me, old boy. See you soon."

Nigel dressed thoughtfully. He wondered if Jean-Claude had come up with something. He'd give him a call, then get right on the *traspaso* thing.

He called Jean-Claude's number. Jean-Claude picked it up on the first ring. They arranged a place to meet in half an hour. Then Nigel dialed Harry Hamm in Ibiza, hoping to find him at El Caballo Negro bar in Santa Eulalia. And while he waited for the phone to engage, he was pursing his lips and sucking at the ends of his mustache and fiddling with his beard and thinking about Max Rosen and the way he was paying Hob, whom he barely knew, twenty or more times what a service was worth. It was something to think about.

19

Aurora packed quickly, choosing the pigskin Samsonite as her main traveling case. She had already canceled her dentist's appointment. Her rent wasn't due for another two and a half weeks. By then she'd have a better idea of how long she would be staying in Paris. Then she'd do what had to be done. Meanwhile, she just had to get there.

She was standing in her beautifully decorated little apartment on East Sixty-sixth Street near East River Drive, wearing a half slip and bra and pink mules and sipping a fortified peach nectar that was said to supply necessary vitamins lost while indulging in illicit narcotics.

The sun was slanting in through the venetian blinds. Outside, Manhattan pulsed, throbbed, and writhed in its customary and inimitable way. Aurora stood in front of the window, tall and slender even in flat mules, long, reddish gold hair that had been likened to that of Rita Hayworth as seen in *The Lady from Shanghai* flung back carelessly over her light brown shoulders. Her full mouth fell naturally into an attractive pout as she said to herself, Okay, baby, now there comes the delicate question of how to handle Emilio.

Emilio was the undercover DEA agent she was dating. They had a date that evening at eight o'clock at the Carnival Bar on West Seventy-second. And Emilio had asked her to come out to Montauk with him this weekend for some fishing. He had the use of some Mafia guy's luxurious cottage. She had more or less agreed to accompany him, but had been having second thoughts ever since. Now, with the Paris trip coming up in the morning, she knew she would have to cancel Montauk and break tonight's date with him. She had things to do. And besides, he was part of her old life and she was about to put all that behind her. But how should she go about breaking the date?

Call him? But she had no idea where to find him before their date this evening. She couldn't call him at DEA headquarters because he didn't know she knew he was undercover DEA. He had introduced himself to her as a well-connected wiseguy with plenty of money and no visible means of support. Should she show up at the Five Points Sporting Club and tell him then? She really didn't want to do that. Emilio had been getting very possessive of late. He was acting like he had some sort of rights over her. She didn't like that. She had been thinking for a while now that it was time to end this thing with Emilio. He had been fun, in his crude, boisterous, faintly sinister way, but it was enough already, as her Jewish girlfriend Sarah Deiter would say.

The more she thought about it, the more uncomfortable she became at the idea of having to tell Emilio in person that she was going out of town. He was too inquisitive. Too pushy. But what the hell, she had to do it.

She went to her closet and started to select an outfit for the meeting, decisive at last.

20

Le Lapin Agile was a small, not very interesting Paris bar with typical Parisian smells of sawdust and black tobacco, stale wine and beer. There were half a dozen people inside, working people from the *quartier.* A soccer game was showing on the black-and-white TV but no one was getting very excited about it. The arrival of the new Beaujolais gave people an excuse to tipple, not that they needed any, life being what it is and alcohol what it is.

Nigel sat outside on the terrace, his overcoat collar turned up against the brisk and unexpected wind. He was beautifully dressed in the sort of Saville Row tweed suit that only gets better as it grows older, and thus is a boon to impecunious gentlemen who can't afford a new wardrobe every year or even every ten years. Nigel was smoking a long cigarette butt he had found in the ashtray when he sat down. When the waiter came, Nigel ordered a demitasse and a carafe of plain water. It was chilly on the terrace, but this was the first time he'd been outside Schumacher's apartment in three days.

Jean-Claude showed up before he finished the cigarette, wearing a baggy blue-and-red sweater over his skinny frame, his dark hair sleeked back in Latin gigolo style, a habitual sneer on his face even while blowing on his hands.

Keeping both hands in his pockets, Jean-Claude dropped into a white ironwork chair. When the waiter came over he ordered a Negroni, and a brandy and coffee for Nigel.

Jean-Claude was broke at this time, too, but not as broke as Nigel. Jean-Claude was eating, at least, though Le Chat Verte served arguably the worst food in Paris. It was a nightclub on one of those sinister little side streets off the rue Blanche in Pigalle. Jean-Claude got one meal a day there in return for keeping the clientele in line and acting as bodyguard for the Iraqi owner, who had a problem with some people sent by the Baathist party back home to teach him some respect. What they were annoyed about had happened long ago. What al-Targi had done to earn their displeasure escaped everyone's recollection. All anyone knew was there was still a score to be settled. But not while Jean-Claude was on shift.

Jean-Claude was not one of your big bruisers. He was about five foot eight, 120 pounds, with stringy muscles and quick reflexes. "What need do I have for muscles?" Jean-Claude used to say. "It takes no great strength to beat up a woman. As for men—a pistol, a knife . . ." He shrugged, the expressive Apache shrug with downturned mouth.

Jean-Claude was a type. Maybe his long-range prospects weren't so good, but so far his mad dog image had stood him in good stead. Like Nigel, he was waiting for something to turn up.

"Good of you, old boy," Nigel said when the drinks came. "Come into an inheritance, have you?"

Jean-Claude shrugged. "Fifi insisted on making me a little loan. But I fear it is the last. She is—how you Britishers say it?—tapped out."

"It's the Americans who say that," Nigel said. "But the meaning is universal. Hob thinks there may be a little dividend soon."

Jean-Claude curled his lower lip in a gesture that meant, I'll believe it when I see it, then winked to show he didn't really mean it.

"About time the agency paid us something for our work. Has he found a wealthy investor?"

"Something like that," Nigel said. "He's escorting a woman from New York to Paris and getting ten thousand dollars for it and a free ticket to De Gaulle."

Jean-Claude made a typically Gallic gesture and said, *"Peste!* I'd like a job like that! Who is he working for?"

"I don't think you met him," Nigel said. "His name is Max Rosen and he spent one summer in Ibiza. But I think you were in Norway that summer with the countess."

"Ah yes, the duchess," Jean-Claude said, kissing his fingertips and rolling his eyes as one who remembers past bounties. "But I came back to Ibiza in time to meet Rosen. I was staying with Allan Darby and Sue, don't you remember?"

"Of course, old boy. I was staying with poor old Elmyr."

"And of course I know about Rosen's agency."

"What do you mean, 'of course'?"

"Is it not obvious," said Jean-Claude, "that when one has an interest in the ladies, it pays to befriend one who employs beautiful young models? I called upon Max Rosen upon the occasion of my visit to New York. He—how do you say it?—fixed me up?"

"Yes, I'm sure that's the word you're looking for," said Nigel.

"Fixed me up with a stunning young black woman who showed me the sights of Harlem."

"Well, this Rosen has hired Hob to locate and escort a young lady back to Paris. And I understand the young lady will not prove hard to find."

"And he is paying ten thousand dollars for this," Jean-Claude said.

"And a one-way ticket to Paris worth another five hundred, over a thousand if it's first-class, as I suspect."

Jean-Claude thought for a while. "It is a lot of money."

"Exactly what I was thinking."

"Too much for an escort. Not enough for a mule."

"I beg your pardon, old boy?"

"A mule," Jean-Claude said, "is a person who carries narcotics through customs on behalf of another person."

"I know what a mule is," Nigel said. "I taught you the term myself. Are you implying that Hob would smuggle narcotics for ten thousand dollars?"

"Certainly not. I believe Hob would not smuggle narcotics again for any price. Not after Turkey. But I think someone might use him. Put something into his suitcase before it goes through customs. It's been done plenty of times."

"Hob would never fall for an old one like that," Nigel said, but he didn't sound entirely certain.

"Hob needs ten thousand for the *traspaso,*" Jean-Claude said. "He's apt to not think too far beyond that, *n'cest pas?*"

"Certainement," Nigel said slowly. "But is there any reason to suspect that this Max, this model agent, is a dope smuggler?"

Jean-Claude shrugged again, a how-should-I-know shrug. "But we could make a few phone calls and see what we could find out."

Nigel threw back his brandy, and then the coffee. He stood up. "I think we should do just that."

21

Aurora and Emilio met at the Carnival Bar. Emilio was there when Aurora arrived. She came into the bar, wearing one of the prettiest traveling suits Emilio had ever seen her in. It had a short jacket that flounced at the hips, and a short skirt revealing her great long skinny model's legs. She wore a little hat with a veil. She looked good enough to eat, but in that cold heartless model way that Emilio found so exciting.

He was a big, strong-looking man in his thirties, this Emilio, and he had blond Irish looks that belied his Hispanic name. He was not very well dressed in a brown gabardine suit that came from Macy's rather than a designer's boutique.

Aurora wasted no time. She could be very straightforward.

"Emilio," she said, "I'm sorry but something has come up. I'm going to be out of town for a while."

Oddly enough, Emilio had been expecting something like that. Still, he feigned an appropriate degree of surprise.

"Oh, really? What's up?"

"I'm going to model in Paris. I've just been sent for."

"Paris, France?"

"That's the one. I leave in the morning."

"Tomorrow morning?"

"Yes. It's crazy, isn't it. But you know how Max is."

"All pretty sudden," he commented. "Anyone seeing you to the airport?"

"As a matter of fact, there is. A private detective Max hired to escort me over."

Emilio whistled softly. "A private detective? Sounds like Max really wants you."

Aurora smiled. "He's such a silly man."

"Well, what can I say? I hate to see ya go. But congratulations, babe. How did Max swing this deal?"

"I really don't know. I think he's been working on it for a long time."

Looking as innocent as possible, Emilio said, "Anything to the rumor that Max is joining up with Dartois?"

Aurora looked at him. "How did you hear about that?"

Emilio shrugged. "You know, word gets out on the street."

"I don't know nothing about Max's business," Aurora said. "But it wouldn't surprise me."

"Well, whatever," Emilio said. "Got time for dinner? Or at least a drink?"

"You know I'd love to," Aurora said, "but I've really got a lot of things to do. I'll call you when I get back. And in the meantime, you can expect a postcard from Paris!"

She gave him a quick kiss on the cheek, made a gallant little wave, and was off. The doorman called a taxi and put her and her suitcase into it. Emilio watched as the taxi drove off. He was smiling, but he wasn't amused.

Emilio finished his drink and paid. He went to the telephone at the end of the bar and made a call. He spoke for a few minutes, then left the bar and took a taxi to the DEA office downtown. On the way he shed his florid tie and rearranged his hair. By the time he reached the office on Worth Street he looked like a normal citizen rather than a street hood with vulgar dress tastes he'd picked up from Mickey Rourke movies.

Lanky, hollow-chested Superintendent Allan Woodrow was in his office when Emilio arrived. Woodrow was drowsing at his desk among the most-wanted bulletins. He looked up when Emilio arrived. "So what's happening, Emilio?"

"The Max Rosen case. It's finally opening up. His girlfriend is going to Paris."

"So?"

"Well, I figure something big is happening."

"Like what?"

"Max is a key dope guy. I figure he's setting up a coke connection in France."

"Maybe. So?"

"This lady of his. She's bound to be bringing in some product for him."

"Well, easy enough to have her searched at French customs."

"She won't be carrying it herself. There's a guy who's going with her. A private detective. He'll be carrying it. It's obvious that's why he's along. To be the mule. And to guard it once the stuff is in Paris."

"You could be right, Emilio. But we don't really know. It's all conjecture, isn't it?"

"I think there's enough cause to alert Paris."

"No problem there. We've been working with them."

"But I don't want them to bust these people at customs. I want them to let them through and put a trace on them. We don't want to arrest some mule. Not after all the time we've put in on this case. We don't even want a girlfriend of a dope dealer. We want Max himself, and some of his associates, higher up if we can get them. We want to see these people handing the dope over to Max."

"You're sure there's going to be dope?"

"Yeah, I'm sure. I've got my contacts. What about it?"

"What about what? We can ask Paris for cooperation. Maybe they'll do the tail, too, if we ask them nice. What else do you want?"

"I want to go there myself. I've been working on Max Rosen for almost two years. I want to be in at the kill."

"Emilio, you don't even speak French!"

"But I know what I'm doing. I don't trust these French not to screw it up. They do that a lot, you know?"

"We screw up some ourselves, Emilio."

"I don't. I'll make sure it goes right. And I want to be in there at the kill."

"Sorry, I can't authorize it."

"Then you can give me some leave time."

"What are you talking about?"

"I've been undercover on this thing for a long time. I have leave time coming up. I'll go to Paris at my own expense."

"Emilio, this is not a good idea."

"Just sign my papers, okay? I'm calling Air France."

22

Nigel and Jean-Claude met again at Le Lapin Agile in the early afternoon.

"Before anything else," Nigel said, "there are a few things we need to do. We need to get our hands on some money. I don't even have a metro ticket. Also, I have an idea."

Jean-Claude: "What is it?"

"Hob flies in tomorrow. He'll be carrying this stuff on him. It's obvious he's being set up. We have to do something about it."

"Telephone him," Jean-Claude suggested. "You can still use the phone in this place where you're staying, *n'cest pas?* Call him and warn him."

"That won't do," Nigel said. "You know Hob. He's a hothead. He'll have it out with whoever he's dealing with on the New York end. They'll scrub the deal, assuming they don't scrub him. Take him out of it. Do it later with someone else."

"Well, what of that? Hob will be safe."

"That's not quite good enough, old boy. The reason Max is paying him so much money to accompany the woman to Paris is so that Hob, wittingly or not, will act as courier. Getting Hob to carry this package to France is the whole point of the operation. If Hob doesn't do it, there'll be no payoff."

"And no money for us," Jean-Claude said thoughtfully.

"It's worse than that, you silly twit. He won't be able to pay off on his finca. He'll lose it."

"Ah," said Jean-Claude. "That would be a pity, of course."

"You bet your boots it would be a pity. Not just for Hob. That finca is ours, too."

"How do you figure?"

"You've heard him say it often enough. The finca is for all of Hob's friends. It belongs to all of us. He means that literally. He sees himself as responsible for providing the place, but he doesn't consider it exclusively his."

"Well then, the finca is ours, too. What of it?"

"That finca is our insurance policy, Jean-Claude, the place we can go when we bust out everywhere else, when we're too feeble to hire out for anything and too old and ugly to attract a woman. It's the place where we can live free the rest of our lives. It's our retirement home, the old soldiers' home, sailors' snug harbor, the only one we'll ever have. Our place in the sun. Ours! Get that into your head. Not just Hob's. Ours, too."

"You're sure of that?"

"You know Hob. You've heard him talk about the agency and the finca enough. What do you think?"

Jean-Claude bent his narrow head with the dark brilliantined hair combed straight back. He made thinking movements with his mouth. His thin knife of a nose twitched. You could almost see the thoughts pouring onto the slate gray computer screens of his eyes. His hand reached out blindly and Nigel slipped one of his last Disque Bleus into it. It was that crucial a moment.

Jean-Claude lit up and blew a thin double plume of smoke through his nostrils. He said, *"Peste!"*

"Exactly," Nigel said.

"I think you are correct in your assessment of Hob's character," Jean-Claude said. "It is *our* place, bought at least in part out of our unpaid wages. And we will lose it if Hob doesn't pay off this *traspaso*. Nigel, we must not lose our place in the sun!"

"Agreed," Nigel said.

"So it is simple. We say nothing, Hob goes through with it, and all is well."

"Not quite so simple," Nigel said. "This Max. I don't know him, but from what I've heard, I distrust him in the extreme."

"What do you think he will do?"

"I don't give a damn what he does. But what I fear is that he stiffs Hob."

"*Comment?*"

"Doesn't pay him."

Jean-Claude considered. His face settled into even more sinister lines than usual. He said, "That would not be wise of him."

"As matters stand, we have no control over the situation. But I think there's something we can do to gain some leverage."

"And what is that?"

"We'll need the assistance of one of your underworld friends."

"Ah," Jean-Claude said.

The Paris underworld is not on the usual tourist beat save for the traditional haunts in Montmartre and Montparnasse. Like the famous monuments and the less well known insane asylums, there are regional centers for organized crime all over the city. The rue Rambuteau has been a favorite ever since the Centre Pompidou was put up. Before that, Les Halles was a traditional area for those battening off the meat and produce industries. The Café Valentine in the place d'Italie is a favorite of Algerian gangsters. Their Vietnamese counterparts hang out at the Café Ho Ha on a street with no name off the avenue d'Ivry close to metro Tolbiac. The Chinese have several cafés of their own not far from there, off the boulevard Massena where it joins Kellerman. Corsican heavies stay away from the Thirteenth, preferring to congregate at the Polo Bar in the place des Vosges. These are the main areas at present writing. In addition there are several international cafés where gangsters of all nationalities are welcome. The best known of these is the Lac d'Or restaurant in Belleville. Here, amid the steaming smells of dim sum, latter-day Apaches and toughs from all over can be sure of a warm welcome. Even the South Americans sometimes come here, forsaking their usual roost in the back room of the restaurant Brazil near the Bourse. It was to the Lac d'Or that Nigel and Jean-Claude repaired.

Their waiter recognized them, but, in his inscrutable way, pretended not to. They were served tea, and ordered a plate of barbecued pork to nibble on while they sized up their surroundings. The Lac d'Or was a place where most of the criminal element put in an appearance at least once a day. It was a cross between a lowlife casting studio and a goniff's hiring hall. Nigel had never been here before, but Jean-Claude was quite familiar with the place. Although he wasn't exactly a criminal himself, Jean-Claude liked criminals and tended to spend a lot of time in their company. He was one of those people who thrive on the appearance of the sinister.

"Remember," Nigel told him, "we need someone we can rely on. No freelancing on this job. He must do exactly what he is told. And above all, no violence. I could never forgive myself if anything happened to Hob."

"Don't worry so much," Jean-Claude said crossly. "I'm looking for one particular person. He'll do exactly as I say."

"What makes you so sure of that?"

"Because he's married to my cousin Sabine. . . . There he is!"

The person Jean-Claude was referring to was a medium-sized man of Arab features with a small, well-trimmed dark beard. Olive skin. Dark, expressive eyes. Dark suit and dark tie. He couldn't have advertised any better with a neon sign. When he saw Jean-Claude, his face lit up. He came over, they shook hands and *ca-va*'ed each other, Nigel was introduced, and the new man, whose name was Habib, sat down and ordered a tea and a plate of egg rolls. Habib and Jean-Claude exchanged family information. Then Jean-Claude got down to it.

"You working these days?"

Habib gave an expressive shrug and a mouth gesture indicating he had seen better days.

"I've got a little job for you."

Raised eyebrows indicating cautious interest.

"You don't get anything out of it but what I pay you."

A nod.

"It's a stickup job."

"Those are more expensive," Habib said automatically.

"Be tranquil, wait until I tell you about it before you try to jack up the price."

Half-closed eyes indicating that he was listening.

"A certain person is arriving at De Gaulle tomorrow evening. Late. We'll need the services also of your cousin the taxi driver."

"Ali will cost extra."

"Will you have the decency to wait and listen to the entire proposition? You'll pick up this fare at De Gaulle. You'll carry a sign with his name. I will also describe him to you. There'll be a woman with him."

Habib made as if to speak. Nigel put in for him, "That'll cost more."

Jean-Claude said, "Your cousin will take them to whatever backstreet in Belleville or Port-Royal that you prefer. You know the district better than I do. You will rob the man of his luggage, but not what is on his person. You will take from his luggage only a certain package which I will describe to you. You will bring it to me, unopened. For this I will pay you five thousand francs."

Habib thought it over, turned it around in his mind, and said, "Ten thousand. And an extra five thousand for Ali."

23

For the next half hour, Hob and Dorrie took turns trying to call Aurora at her apartment. They got her answering machine, but not Aurora herself. A call to the photo studio where she was working that week didn't find her, either. No one knew where she was.

Finally Dorrie had an idea. "There's this place she mentioned downtown, where she works out sometimes."

"Downtown where?"

"It's in Chinatown."

"Where she works out? What do you mean, works out?"

"Exercises. Hatha yoga, I think it is called."

It seemed to Hob that Dorrie's expression made it plain that she wouldn't be interested in putting her own body through anything that sweaty and strenuous. Not in public, anyhow.

"Can we call them?" Hob asked.

"I'm not sure of the name. But I know it's on Mott just in from Canal."

They left Kelly in Max's apartment, sitting in the kitchenette and drinking beer, ready to answer the phones in case Aurora should call in. They caught a taxi within half a block of the apartment.

The Five Points Gaming Club was located above a big Chinese grocery on Canal near the corner of Mott and Pell Streets. Hob and Dorrie walked through the grocery, past the piles of bok choy and winter melon, past Chinese housewives in black silk pants and flowering tops and stiff Mandarin collars embroidered with crimson thread, arguing the price of mandrake root with wiry old men with faces like wrinkled oranges; and all the while children played in the aisles and chewed on strips of barbecued beef. A fat Chinese man pushed a broom over the sawdust-scattered floor as the big fans turned slowly overhead. The warm moist summer air was heavy with the odors of salted shrimp and bêche-de-mer.

"You sure this is the right place?" Hob asked.

Dorrie shrugged. "The entrance to the club is right behind here."

Hob and Dorrie went to the back of the grocery, past the barrels of shark fins and the bins of white-veined green cabbages, past the jars of hoisin sauce and the tall tapering bottles of imported soy sauce from Hong Kong, to a door marked Private and Privileged that led to a flight of stairs. At the end of a dusty corridor was a door with a sign reading Five Points Athletic and Gaming Club.

Inside, Hob saw a boxing ring in the center of a large room, with two Oriental boys sparring with big red gloves. Hob tried to remember if there had ever been any great Chinese boxers, but couldn't think of one. The place smelled of sweat and tangerine peel. In another part of the room, several tables had been set up with fan-tan and mah-jongg layouts. There were people seated around these tables. As Hob had suspected, the Five Points Gaming Club was a cover for an old-style gambling place. At a third table four players, two of them Caucasian, or perhaps Semitic, or a mixture, were playing bridge.

Dorrie and Hob drifted over to the bridge table. The players continued playing with elaborate unconcern. After about five minutes, one of the players, a Chinese, said, "Kin we help you, bub?" He had the longest fingernails Hob had ever seen outside of a Fu Manchu movie.

"Is there a Mr. Horner here?" Dorrie asked. To Hob, she said, "That's who Aurora told me to ask for."

The Chinese fellow jerked his thumb toward the far corner of the room. Hob saw a white man in black shorts and a pocketless white T-shirt slapping away at a speed bag. He looked like a middleweight, though Hob was no expert on these matters. He was about five foot nine, with heavy sloping shoulders and a thickening waist. He had a tough New York face of the snub-nosed variety. Hob sensed immediately that he and the boxer would never be really close friends.

As they approached him, Dorrie and Hob exchanged glances. In one of those psychic moments that sometimes occur in even the worst of relationships, they decided silently that it would be better if Dorrie handled this one.

Dorrie walked up to the boxer, Hob trailing, and said, "Mr. Horner? I'm Dorrie Tyler of Max Rosen Associates. This is Mr. Draconian, my associate."

"Pleased ta meetcha," Horner said, not looking pleased at all.

"We are trying to locate Miss Aurora Sanchez," Dorrie continued. "A very important modeling job has come up for her. It would not be an exaggeration to say that this job could make her rich and famous. But we need to know if she wants the job, and we need an answer rather quickly, otherwise someone else will be chosen. Can you help us find her?"

Jack Horner looked hard at Dorrie, then at Hob. His frown drew his eyebrows together like a Do Not Trespass sign written in hairy cuneiform.

"I gotta shower and dress," he said. "Then, okay, yeah, I think I can help ya."

"You see?" Dorrie said, after he had gone away to shower. "When you talk nice to people, you get results."

Hob liked a woman who was not afraid to say "I told you so." As it turned out, Dorrie was wrong. But that was only to be expected.

Jack Horner did not impress Hob any more dressed than he had wearing boxing trunks. He had one of those flat little hats like

Gene Hackman wore in *The French Connection*—a hat that would make you look like an idiot even if you were Socrates and Einstein rolled into one. Add to this that Horner was wearing a sort of knit jacket in white and black and orange, the sort of thing that only a color-blind pug suffering from an extreme case of vulgaritis could have picked. But of course, on Canal Street it didn't seem too weird an outfit.

"Where are we going?" Dorrie asked, once they were on the street.

"You want Aurora?" Horner said. "I got to show you something."

"What is it?"

"Hey, I'm showing it to you, ain't I?"

On a person like Horner, "ain't" didn't sound illiterate; it sounded like a word from the undecipherable language of a tribe that hated you.

Horner hurried them down Canal to White Street. They turned left past the little park, with the East River beyond it opening into New York Bay. It was another country entirely, that bay, and the other bays like it, that made up the misty fen-haunted world of aquatic New York. They came to 125 White Street. It was a restaurant named Grocetti's, and Horner stopped. "Here, here's the place." Without another word he turned on his heel and left.

Andrew, a waiter at Grocetti's, remembered that Aurora had been in about half an hour ago.

"Sure, of course I remember her," he said. He was a tall, delicate-looking young man with an elaborate hairdo and a prominent Adam's apple. "She comes in here once, twice a week for a tequila sunrise, meets some friends."

"Do you have any idea where she's gone?" Hob asked.

Andrew thought long and hard. His brow creased with concentration. Hob finally helped him along with one of Max's twenties.

"She's probably gone to Doris Castillo's party," he said at

last. "It's the sort of event she wouldn't miss."

"Where's that?"

"One-oh-one Duane Street."

"What apartment number?"

He shrugged. "You get there, you'll see for yourself which apartment."

The waiter was correct: there was no trouble finding Doris Castillo's party. It was in a part of Tribeca normally deserted except for meat-packers and their friends. But now, cars and limos were parked all up and down the block. Hand-lettered signs on the front of the building pointed the direction. A press car from one of the cable networks was present.

They rode up to Doris Castillo's apartment in a freight elevator with two men in tuxedos. The elevator opened onto a room about the size of a football field. There were about a thousand people present, give or take a few hundred. Scattered around the room were workbenches filled with sculptures in various stages of completion, running the gamut from bare armatures to completed busts. There were flashing and winking exhibits of neon art. There were six-foot cardboard crayons and gigantic cardboard packs of Lucky Strikes. There was a buffet table loaded with good things. Hob helped himself to an open-faced turkey-and-avocado sandwich on black seed rye. He was pretty sure the rye came from Zabar's. He found a Negro Modelo and poured half of it into a paper cup. While he was doing that, Dorrie was circulating. She came back after a short while with a tall, very attractive girl with a great head of reddish gold hair and a neat, engaging smile. "Hob," Dorrie said, "I want you to meet Aurora Sanchez. Aurora, this is Hob Draconian." And so the search was over.

24

Aurora Sanchez was wearing a simple, beautifully cut black evening dress, off the shoulders. Around her neck, which was long and shapely, though not quite long enough to be described as swanlike, she wore a finely woven gold chain from which depended a little jade figure. Hob caught a glimpse of gold bead earrings. Her dress came to midcalf, a fashionable length that year, no doubt. She had on black patent leather high heels. She carried a little gold mesh purse. She wore no rings. She was prettier in person than her publicity stills. There was an openness and good humor to her features that Hob hadn't expected. Her complexion was very good if you like that light golden tawny look. She held herself very erect. She was taller than he had expected, five foot ten at least. Her slimness and erect stature made her look even taller.

"Is this about the job in Paris?" she asked at once. She had a deep voice, faintly flavored with vodka and Spanish.

Hob told her what Max had told him about the job in Paris and the necessity of being on the morning flight.

"Model of the year!" Dorrie said. "Oh, Aurora, it's wonderful!"

Aurora was beaming. The two girls began to talk about what Aurora should pack for Paris. Hob found it not unpleasant to listen to two pretty women chatter about their wardrobes. Still, time was of the essence. And now a small but disturbing thought crossed Hob's mind.

"Will it take you much time to get ready?" he asked Aurora. "We've got a flight at seven in the morning."

"I can be packed in half an hour," Aurora said. "But I do have to pick up something first."

"Want me to come along?" Hob asked, not wanting to lose sight of this person worth ten thousand dollars delivered live tomorrow in Paris.

"Sure. I'd appreciate it."

Dorrie said, "Okay, I'm going back to the apartment. Meet you both there. Kelly will take us out to Kennedy."

Aurora said, "I've got to make a quick call. Be right back."

Dorrie left. Hob found himself near one of the appetizer tables. He made inroads into the caviar, sampled the Swedish meatballs, munched a few cheese puffs, and washed it all down with a glass of white wine. He was feeling pretty good. The ten grand bonus was practically his. It hadn't been so difficult after all.

Aurora came back in a few minutes. "Let's go!"

25

Aurora's little car was parked around the corner on West Broadway. It was a red Porsche 911, not new but recent, very dusty and very classy. They got in and Aurora turned north on Sixth Avenue.

"Do you work for Max?" she asked.

"I'm a private detective," Hob told her.

"You don't really look much like a private detective."

"I didn't have time to put on my makeup."

"Have you known Max long?"

"About ten years. Met him in Ibiza. Ever been there?"

"With my parents, about twelve years ago. We stayed at a friend's house in Santa Gertrudis. And once on my own, about four years ago. I stayed in Formentera that time. Does Formentera count?"

There were four Balearic Islands situated in the western Mediterranean between France and Spain. Majorca was the big one, Ibiza was the crazy one, Minorca was the English one, and Formentera, which lies just a mile or two away from Ibiza, was the sun worshiper's island, where freaks went to get away from other freaks.

"Sure it counts," Hob said. He was about to ask her how she liked the place and whether she was going back again soon—like immediately after Paris, and perhaps in company with a private detective—when she said, "Do you have a gun?"

"A gun? You mean do I own one?"

"I don't care if you own one or not. Do you have one on you right now?"

"No, I don't. Is it important?"

"Probably not," she said.

"Do you think we might need a gun?"

"Might."

"What makes you think so."

" 'Cause we're being followed."

Hob looked back. Just then Aurora saw a break in the traffic and whipped her car out into it. Never assume, as Hob had done, that a pretty girl driving a Porsche doesn't know anything about handling a car. Pretty girls often have hoodlum boyfriends who show them the basics of high-speed driving. She wound the little car up through its gears. There were quite a few gears, four or five at least. She made a turn and raced downtown, swung around the Fulton Fish Market like it was a pylon and she a racing airplane, and headed back uptown on Church Street. The Porsche howled like a banshee and clung to the road like a leech. Looking back, Hob saw that the car behind them had made that mad turn, too, and was in hot pursuit. As it came under the streetlights Hob saw that it as a white late-model Mercedes. He couldn't tell how many people were in it, but they were coming on fast.

"Shit," Aurora said, "they told me this wouldn't happen."

She dropped down a gear and swung unexpectedly around a corner. She was skillful, but she took up all the road. It was lucky traffic was light. The Mercedes barreled out of Gansevoort Street and followed onto Greenwich Avenue. It was coming up on them fast. As usual when you get into a jam, there was not a cop in sight. Aurora made another turn onto Eighth Street, clipping the curb and rocking up giddily on two wheels. The Mercedes was being driven by someone who knew how. He kept right on behind them.

"Do you at least know how to use a gun?" she asked.

"When I have to, I can."

"There's one in the glove compartment. You may have to."

Hob got it out. It was a Lugery sort of gun, black and with a long slender snout. Hob felt a little foolish holding it, especially since he wasn't sure how it worked. He didn't even know how many safety catches it had. While he was figuring it out, the Mercedes roared up alongside. Hob never heard the shots above the roar of the cars' engines, but two neat holes appeared in the windshield.

"Hey," he said, "what have you gotten us into?"

"Don't panic," she said. "Watch this."

She kept the Porsche in a low gear—second, third, who knows about such things?—as they proceeded at speed on Broadway. The Mercedes was trying to come up on them again. "Hang on," Aurora said, and braked hard and swung the wheel and hit the accelerator. She put the car into as nice a bootlegger's turn as Hob had ever seen outside of likker-running movies. The Porsche slewed around in a four-wheel drift, its engine ranting and raving like a hysterical orator trying to make a point, and somehow came around 180 degrees and ended up facing downtown. The Mercedes slewed around and was coming toward them again and Aurora neatly evaded it and ran away while the Mercedes banged against a couple of parked cars and had to slow down to regain its composure. And then the Mercedes was out of sight and they cut across town to St. Mark's Place, then north on First Avenue, past Bellevue. The Mercedes was nowhere around.

Aurora drove west to Second Avenue and pulled over to the curb at Sixteenth Street. set the emergency brake, and leaned back with a deep sigh.

"You done good," Hob said.

"Yeah." She smiled seriously. "When you're good, you're good. Have you a cigarette?"

A cigarette is of course de rigueur after a high-speed car chase. In fact, that's just about the only time Hob smoked after recently giving up tobacco. He fished out a Ducado, one of his few remaining Spanish cigarettes.

She took it, her hands shaking as she lit it. She blew out smoke and said, "Look, you might as well know it, I've got problems."

26

Luke's Forget-Me-Not Good Eats 24 Hours a Day was located on Sixteenth Street near Second. It was a garish place, all neon and colored lights and mirrors and artificial flowers. There was a huge Wurlitzer pounding out the sentimental 1940s favorites that Moishe, the owner, preferred since they are what he had listened to on the kibbutz at Ein Klein the year before he emigrated to America. The waitresses were your standard industrial models, with blondined hair, wet lipstick that glowed in the dark, and pink uniforms that concealed sweaty misshapenness. Aurora ordered coffee and buttered toast.

"Now look," Hob said, "just what in hell is going on?"

"It's a long story," Aurora said. "I don't know where to begin. I don't even know how to explain Paco."

"Begin with Max. Did he set me up for this?"

"You have a very suspicious nature," she said. "I assure you, Max knows nothing."

"What's this with Paco you mentioned?"

She hesitated. Her lower lip protruded slightly in one of the cutest moues of the year. "He's sort of involved, in a way. But it's complicated."

"And a long story, as you've already noted."

"Look," Aurora said, her tone suddenly no-nonsense, "I have to pick up something and deliver it to someone. There's no way around it, I have to."

"Couldn't it wait until after Paris?"

"I have to do it tonight."

"That sounds reasonable enough," Hob said. "But it is becoming obvious that someone doesn't want you to do it."

"Yes."

"If you keep on trying, you could get killed."

"Yes."

"So could I."

She gave a brave little smile. "I'm not afraid."

"Well, I am."

The brave little smile faded from her lips, to be replaced by a much less pretty expression of contempt. "You're really a coward, aren't you?"

"Yes, though I fail to see what that has to do with it. The point is, why should I stick my neck out for you? My job was to find you and bring you to Paris. Nobody said anything about having to cope with a Mercedes full of gunmen for the same price."

"I guess not," she said, sighing. "You've done what you agreed to do."

"Not exactly. I still have to get on a plane with you tomorrow morning."

"What happens if you don't?"

"Then I don't get my bonus."

"Is it a big bonus?"

It crossed Hob's mind to tell her the bonus was insignificant. After all, why tell the truth when a lie will serve better? Having decided this, it surprised Hob to hear himself say, "If ten thousand dollars is big, it's a big bonus."

She thought about that for a while, doodling on a napkin with an eyebrow pencil. Without looking up at him she said, "Hob, I need your help."

Hob's heart leaped at the words, but the wizened dwarf in his head who had to pass on all matters of sentiment kept him under control.

"Why should I help you? It's true that you're lovely and desirable, but even if you were planning on going to bed with me, which I doubt, we're unlikely to live long enough to accomplish it."

"I am not going to bed with you," she said. "But if you help me, I will pay you."

"Handsomely?" Hob asked.

"Yes, handsomely."

"Okay, now let's forget handsomely and talk real money. How much to help you do your errand?"

She pondered. "It's just one night's work."

"In which I could be killed," Hob reminded her.

"How does five hundred dollars sound?"

"A little less than handsome, given the circumstances."

"A thousand?"

"A thousand, and a full explanation of what's going on."

"What about two thousand and no explanation?"

"Let's say two thousand and an explanation, but you can lie and I'll pretend not to notice."

"Two thousand dollars! It's unethical of you to put up the price that way."

"It's not going to come out of your pocket, is it?"

"That has nothing to do with the ethics of the matter," she said stiffly.

"I'm afraid you've been watching too many private eye movies. Especially the sort in which the tough old private eye helps out the beautiful young lady just because she needs help. Actually, when the client is in distress, that's when our product is most in demand, and it's logical for the price to go up accordingly, according to the capitalistic system we live in which permits this sort of thing."

"Do other detectives think like you?"

"Probably not. But I'm trying to start a trend."

She sighed. Women tended to sigh a lot around Hob. "Okay. We have a deal. You were only kidding about not knowing how to use the Luger, weren't you?"

"You'll just have to show me how to load it and work the

safeties. I can figure out the rest for myself."

"All right. Deal." She held out her hand.

Hob took it in both of his. "Before we shake on it, there remains the tiny question of money. What would be nice would be if you could manage the entire fee in advance in case one of us gets killed tonight."

Money! She looked at Hob as if he'd said a dirty word. Funny how beautiful women hate to lay out money even if it isn't their own.

"Do you take traveler's checks?" she asked.

"American Express or Barclay's," Hob replied.

She pulled a slim wallet from her purse and signed over four five-hundred-dollar checks. Hob put them away in his wallet. This was going to help set up the Alternative Detective Agency, assuming he lived to cash them.

Just then Paco came through the door, recognized Aurora, and came over to the table. It was late in the evening when the meeting finally took place. Probably around 10:00 P.M. Dotty Sayers, a waitress at Luke's Forget-Me-Not Diner, remembered seeing the three of them:

"Two guys and a woman. A beautiful woman, really a peach. I used to be quite a peach myself. That was before I had my trouble with the water thing. I guess you heard about that. That's why you're interviewing me, isn't it? No? Well, never mind, these three people, they were in that last booth over there. I distinctly remember the tall man, not really tall but taller than the other guy, the one you tell me now was Hob Draconian. He was flipping the entries of that jukebox thing. He wanted to play something, but he couldn't find just what he wanted. There were over a hundred selections, so it took him some time to look through them all. At last he found this old Crosby Stills Nash number. 'Our House' or some such sentimental shit as that. Two cats in the yard. Wooden ships. That sort of a number. The sort of thing they put in strictly for the old-timers. And this Hob person sort of settled back while the woman, Aurora, you called her, talked with Paco, the Indian-looking fellow. And I guess they talked awhile because they were still there when I looked at them again about fifteen minutes later. I was busy with a double manicotti and there was a funny thing about that. You don't want to hear about it? All right, you don't need to shout. No, I didn't actually see the package change hands. I saw Paco take out something, but he had a scarf wrapped around it. It looked like a cashmere scarf to me, or possibly camel hair, and it was wrapped around something, something rectangular, or do I mean oblong, and then one of them took the package. I think it was the man. Yes, it was the man. No, wait, the woman reached for it.

"And I heard the man, Hob, heard him say, 'Are you sure you weren't followed?' And Paco said, 'I think not, why?' And Hob said, 'Because that gray Oldsmobile with the broken radio antenna has been around the block three times.' And Aurora looked at him sort of admiringly and she said, 'You notice things like that, don't you?' And Hob said, 'It's my business, lady.' Which I thought was very butch."

Dotty went on: "It was going hell-bent for ten o'clock when Aurora paid the check and they left the diner and stepped out into the murderous cacaphony of a weary whore of a New York night. The streets were full of a tinsel splendor in which hip Jamaicans in porkpie hats with skinny brims played three-card monte with loinweary damsels from the sisterhood of endless night. From neighboring bars and bistros came the sound of Dixieland, hot and dirty, just like they brought it up the river from New Orleans or down the river from Chicago, depending on your orientation. Crack dealers stood in dim satanic doorways selling their vile drug to dwarves with flower faces. A multichanging manycolored stream of people poured by like an endless pride of lions. Paco and Aurora met and exchanged the package. And then the three of them went out the door and that's when the gunfire started. The dark city streets. The streetlights. Long-legged shadows running down the streets lit by sinister streetlights of a steamy whore of a night with a touch of rain in the air and that smell of mayhem and decay that never leaves this queen whore of all the whore cities in the whoring universe. Sure, I saw the two men, but for me they had no features, they were nothing but shadows monstrously elongated like dream images on a nightmare canvas, or like something out of *The Third Man.* Hob was running ahead of them, and the woman was running with him. Her high heels clattered on the damp pavement, and lights from the nearby construction site picked out dazzling highlights in her intricate web of hair. Paco was bringing up the rear, but he abruptly dodged off into a side street. The two guys who were in pursuit ignored him. They were after Hob and the girl. And then the girl peeled off and took off on her own. She shouted something to Hob but he didn't hear it. *'Bon chance,'* maybe.

"The two pursuers hesitated, looked at each other, and some sort of a signal must have passed between them. Or maybe one said something to the other. If so, Hob didn't hear it because just then the mother of all garbage trucks came rumbling past and when the sound environment had cleared up, the girl was gone and you couldn't even hear her clattering high heels anymore. That left Hob all by his lonesome with two guys coming at him deadly, and he kept on running until he came to a dead-end alley. Then he turned, and the pursuers, seeing they had him trapped, slowed down to an ominous tread and then came forward slowly. Hob could see winks of blued steel in their fists. Guns, what else could it be? And I strained forward trying to hear what they were saying, but I couldn't make it out."

27

Trapped. No place to go. One guy on one side of him, the other on the other side of him. All three of them breathing hard. Around them, the dark New York night. Aurora gone. Trouble.

"Stand and deliver," Hob said.

"What?" said the taller of the two men with guns.

"That's what highwaymen used to say to the people they waylaid. 'Stand and deliver.' It meant, give us your money and valuables."

"Ain't that fascinating?" Tall Gunman remarked to his sidekick, a shorter man who wore, among other things, a red bow tie.

"Interesting what you can learn on this job," Bow Tie said.

"If you don't want me to stand and deliver," Hob said, "then we've no business together, so if you'll excuse me . . ."

Bow Tie smiled and said, "I'm Fric and he's Frac. We're traveling hit men. We're different from other people."

"Oh, really?" Hob replied. It wasn't much. He was hoping to stall long enough for his repartee to return.

"Oh yes," Fric said. "Did you think that professional hit men lived in houses with lawns and wives and children like ordinary citizens? Frac and I live in rented rooms above unkempt bars with neon signs that flash on and off in the lonely darkness of the misery of great cities. Sleaze is our milieu, squalor our future, filth our dreams. Aesthetically, it's not really a living. But it is fair enough to say that we hit men are the jackals of the underworld. We drag down the bucks marked for destruction."

Frac, towering bulbous beside his hateful little sidekick, peered down at Hob and said, "I hate guys like you. You think you're so good just because you don't gouge and injure people like we do. As if that meant anything *sub species aeteritatis!* What about the do-badders? Don't you think badness has an equally crucial part to play in the cosmic harmony that rules all things?"

"I never thought about it that way," Hob said. In fact he had, often, but he wasn't going to tell him that.

"Well, think about it," Frac went on. "There's no on without an off. No up without a down. No good without an equal admixture of bad."

Hob listened patiently to what he considered no more than rudimentary Manichaeism. By moving his neck from side to side, as though it were as stiff as it in fact was, but never taking his hopefully hypnotic gaze off Frac's perspiring doughnut face, Hob could take in with his peripheral vision an impression of the warehouse space they had pushed him into, seeing it dimly like a cathedral ornamented with fallen seagulls and old condoms.

"The media portrayal of the philosophical position of a lawbreaker is truly deplorable," Fric put in.

"Unsympathetic portraits?" Hob asked.

"Worse than that." Fric stuck out his lower lip. "They insinuate that our position is morally indefensible."

"Well . . . no offense meant, but isn't it?"

"No, dummy, the existence of the bad is necessary for the existence of the good. Therefore bad is a condition of the good and can't be bad in its own right. Get it?"

"Oh, yes! Yes!"

"You're lying. But what does it matter? Cowardice always accompanies you representatives of the good."

"Be reasonable. I never claimed to be good. And anyhow, what kind of discussion is it when you have the gun?"

"Yeah, I have the gun." Fric regarded the gun for a moment.

"To be philosophically rigorous I ought to turn the gun over to you to show you that your cowardice is innate, not a matter of who's got the weapons."

"That would be an interesting demonstration."

"But I'm not really a philosopher. I'm just a professional hit man who likes to keep intellectually alert. But I suppose we should get on with it. Are final prayers part of your cultural heritage or can we skip the anthropomorphizing?" He raised the gun.

"Hey, come on!" Hob cried, as he struggled with the incompatible emotions of outrage and alarm. "Aren't you going to give me a chance to pray?"

"To an extent," Frac said. "We, too, are creatures of convention. You have thirty seconds." He looked at his watch. Fric drew his gun. Then looked sheepish.

"Actually we weren't going to kill you yet. Don't jump the gun, fella. Just come with us."

28

Hob looked around. This dilapidated warehouse must have put up its For Rent or Sale sign shortly after Cheops put up Big Number One. Antiquity clung to the place like a bat clings to ivy. Depending from the ceiling were ancient joists and battered old trusses and other construction members, and many other things that were lying around the endless expanse of filthy floor like a perverted child's massive toys. The ceiling had been partially destroyed, and now oily-winged seagulls flew in and out like larks of death flocking to a hanging. Even given all this, it would be hard to indicate the intensity of the feelings of dread that this place aroused in Hob except to note that his emotions on first reading "The Pit and the Pendulum" were piddling in comparison.

They went through to an inner room, recently constructed by the look of the wood shavings on the floor and the smell of fresh paint. Fric closed the door and locked it.

Now he could get a better look at his captors. One was a gross fat man with a lardy white face punctured by sparse black bristles, wearing a brown derelict's suit with a necktie pulled tightly around a frayed and dirty collar of forlorn pretensions. His partner (this inference was justifiable, given the stage setting and the postures of the participants), was a skinny little wretch with a hateful face and a twist in his back, reminiscent of that hateful beggar in Browning's Childe Roland, whose crutch traces the letters of doom.

"Where am I?" Hob asked.

"That would be telling," said Fric. He was the skinny malevolent one, and it was strange to see him without his sidekick, the large, gross, thick-necked, bull-biceped triceratops of a man who went by the innocuous name of Frac. Hob was in need of good signs. What he had at present wasn't so great. Hob's feelings were made no better by the room he was in. It was a low-ceilinged, dismal granddaddy of a death-and-anxiety room. It was a cellar of some sort, with a poured concrete floor, or possibly it was a faked poured concrete floor but had actually been built by tiny mollusks rather than the more macroscopic process of laying concrete.

Hob must have said some of that aloud because Fric reacted with a grimace and Frac said, "Acting crazy isn't going to get you out of here."

"Was I acting crazy?" Hob said, leering madly. "I wasn't aware of it. Beg your pardon, I'm sure, hee, hee."

"Stop doing that," Fric said. "Otherwise I'm going to have to mete out some dolorous punishment."

"How well you said that!" Hob said. "Anyone could see at a glance that you are well beyond the gangster class. Would you mind getting me a drink of water? It's hard for me to swap gags with you while my throat is parched."

Fric brought him a glass of water. Frac pulled up a chair and sat down. Fric wore a small derby. It was tilted belligerently over his eyes. His thin white face was bisected by a thin mustache. Something seemed to be bothering him. "I'll be right back," he said, and hurried out the door.

Frac said, "Enough fun. Where's the package?"

"What package?" asked Hob.

Frac said, "Oh, it's going to be that way, is it? Listen, there's no time for fooling around. We want the package that Paco gave to Aurora."

"Why don't you talk to them about it?" Hob said.

"We intend to," Frac said. "Where can we find Aurora?"

"I have no idea. You didn't give us time to set up a rendezvous."

"That's unbelievable. Where is she?"

"I don't know," Hob said, hoping to get conviction into what was only a simple statement of the truth.

"You know what's going to happen when Aziz gets here, don't you?"

Just then the door opened. Fric came in, frowning, small and worried, looking like a Toulouse-Lautrec out of a nightmare. He was carrying a cellular telephone.

"Come with me," he said to Frac. "We've got something to straighten out."

"What about him?" Frac said, indicating Hob with a jerk of his thumb.

"He'll keep. This is important."

"We'll take care of you later, wise guy," Frac said. He left the room with Fric. The door closed and Hob heard the padlock snick into place.

29

IT WAS A bare room, aside from a broken shovel in one corner and a pile of white ashes in a bucket in another. The only door was made of boilerplate. No keyhole. No hinges in sight, either. Hob decided to save his breakout skills for a more auspicious occasion. He looked around. Desk, calendar on the wall, chairs, overhead fluorescent, flickering nastily. He opened the desk.

In the bottom right-hand drawer there was a cellular phone.

He lifted the receiver. Dial tone! Yeah. He gently put it down again.

Now he had a telephone. But who to call? Jerry Raintree? Jerry was almost adequate as a divorce lawyer. But to get him out of a hole like this? Forget it.

Mylar was impossible, even if she was still in town.

He could call 911. Report a combined fire, break-in, civil emergency, and murder. The murder would come later, when the cops found he had put them to all this trouble just because, as far as they could see, he had gotten himself locked into a basement room. If he told them the whole story, he didn't need a lawyer to tell him he'd be charged as an accessory to whatever crimes these goniffs were in the act of perpetrating. His hands weren't exactly clean, either.

If he did call the cops, the best probable outcome would be months of delay while they kept him in New York. Examining the case, they might charge him with a crime. Hell, he was probably guilty of one crime or another. He needed to watch his step or he could end up in jail. And then what about his trip to Paris, his fee, his *traspaso?*

Then he got an idea and on impulse lunged at the telephone and punched in a series of numbers. If there was one thing he knew, it was the direct dialing code for Ibiza. At last a voice came on the other end.

"El Caballo Negro, Sandy speaking."

"This is Hob Draconian," he said.

"Hob, I say! How very nice! Did you know it's five in the morning?"

"So why are you still there?"

"The Mosleys hired the bar for a private party and half the town's here."

Hob could picture Sandy standing there, a tall, very skinny Irishman with a long nose and the finest collection of sweaters in the Balearics.

"I'm in a kind of a hurry," Hob said. "Is Harry Hamm there by any chance?"

"Let me just take a look," Sandy said. Through the receiver Hob could hear the blare of Sandy's cassette player, and the multilingual susurrus of conversation from around the bar. He could picture the place. A two-story whitewashed building. On the outside, the sign, El Caballo Negro, on the black double doors. You went in and two steps down. There was a big pillar in the middle of the room separating the bar into two unequal parts. To the right, a staircase led up to Sandy's quarters—two tiled rooms and a bathroom. Downstairs to the right was the bar, with the bottles behind it. There were rattan and wicker chairs scattered here and there, and low varnished tables. On the walls were photographs of friends, most of them now departed. Hob wanted to be there then, sitting on one of the rickety barstools, a Coke with plenty of ice in his hand, chatting up some English bird who thought our little island quaint beyond words.

"Hob?" Sandy came back on the line. "He's not here. Take a message?"

Hob tried to phrase it in his head. "I am being held prisoner in the basement of some terrible place in New York." Sandy would think he was kidding if he said something like that.

"Tell Harry I have some big-sized money for him," Hob said. "Only there's something he has to do like super-quick to get it."

"Okay, Hob, I got it." Sandy was unruffled by the big news.

"Is there anyone around who could find Harry for me?"

"Let me just check. . . . Tailend Charlie is here."

"Is he sober?"

"Not especially."

"Who else is there?"

"Eddie Buns is here and reasonably sober. And Moira just came in. And wait a minute, speak of the devil . . ."

The next voice was a gruff Jersey City voice. "Hob? You there?"

"Harry, I got something to tell you."

"You got something to tell me? I got something to tell you. I quit."

"Harry, what's the matter?"

"This is no way to run a detective agency. It isn't even a good way to run a funny farm, which is what your operation is starting to look like. What in hell are you doing, hanging around in New York? There's work to be done. When you talked me into this scheme of yours—"

"Harry," Hob said, breaking in. "I'd love to hear the entire bit, but at some other time. Right now I got two things to tell you. Listening?"

"Hob, get back here. I've got something important for us. When can you get here?"

"Harry," Hob said, "it's just possible I'll never make it. In that case, the Alternative Detective Agency is yours. You'll find the papers in the candy box on my desk in the finca. I'll expect you to take care of Nigel and Jean-Claude."

"Stop talking crazy. What kind of trouble you in?"

"It's a little difficult to explain. I started out trying to find someone, tell her about a job, and put her on a plane."

"Straightforward enough so far," Harry said.

"I'm bringing back some money to Ibiza to start our agency with."

"Fine. So why aren't you here already?"

"I was coming to that," Hob said. "I am being held prisoner in a warehouse in New York City at 232A Reade Street. Got that?"

"You're not kidding, are you, Hob? From anyone else I would expect this to be a joke, but from you . . ."

"I'm not kidding, this is the straight goods. I gotta talk fast, Harry. They left me in this room with a live phone but I don't know how long I have before they come back."

"Come back and do what?"

"With luck, just beat me up so badly that I'm a cripple for life. Of course, I might not get off that easy."

"What have you done to them?"

"They say that I've ripped them off of about a million dollars' worth of product."

"So give it back."

"It's a little more complicated than that. Believe me when I tell you that if there were any way of replacing it, I'd be all for that. But it's not in my hands."

"So what is in your hands?"

"This telephone. That's all I've got."

"Hob, this isn't really happening, is it?"

"Goddamn it, Harry, this is not a gag or a stunt."

"All right. Just a second. All right. Give me the info again. Where's that warehouse?"

Hob gave him the whole thing again.

"Okay," Harry said. "I guess there's no time to hear the whole story now. You'd just lie about it anyhow."

"What are you going to do?" Hob asked.

"That's what I'm thinking about," Harry said. "It's a little difficult to be decisive with us three thousand miles apart. All right, I think I got an idea. You're a prisoner in this warehouse, right?"

"That's what I've been trying to say."

"Okay, I got an idea."

"Okay," Hob said. And heard the rattling sound as someone started opening the outside door.

"Gotta go," he said into the phone. "Harry, save me!" He hung up, replaced the phone in the drawer, and stood up to meet his destiny as he'd lived all of his life, erect and proudly whining.

30

THE OUTSIDE DOOR opened. Fric and Frac returned.

Frac said to Fric, "Relax, I'll take care of this."

And suddenly there was Frac. Grinning. Flexing his muscles. Anticipating the pleasure he was going to have grinding Hob's bones into a thin grayish paste. Pausing to savor the various mental bits that went to make up a dream dismembering of a sadistic nature so gross that one could do no more than allude to it. Nor could Hob blame him. Nietzsche once remarked that he hated the weaklings who thought they were good because they had soft paws. In relation to Frac, Hob had soft paws. Naturally he was on the side of the underdog; that was because he was one himself. Judged impersonally, there was no reason to prefer his interpretation over Frac's. But of course, even weaklings with soft paws occasionally have their day.

Hob thought at that dire moment of his guru. His guru was a small Belgian fellow with a big head and preposterous mustaches who taught karate and other skills. This was at the Big Dojo in Ibiza, on the seaward side of the hill. It was a whitewashed building of one story, set into the side of the hill. The place was neither heated nor air-conditioned. There were about ten regulars who attended, breaking bricks with their foreheads and talking esoterically. There were a couple of kids from town who wanted to learn karate so they could compete in karate matches. And there was Hob, trying to learn a skill to keep him from getting killed or beaten up in his chosen work of detectiving.

He never got the hang of it. Any of it.

He asked his instructor, after one particularly exasperating session on the mat when he saw that he'd never get beyond the beginner's white belt, "Isn't there some fighting art that does not require training?"

Hob's guru smiled. "The finest art of all, beyond karate and aikido, beyond ninjitsu, is sun li, the art of the unpremeditated attack. It requires no training. In fact, training destroys its efficacy."

"That sounds like the one for me," Hob said.

"In order to employ it, a man's heart must be pure, and his mind empty."

"My mind is often empty," Hob said. "But pure heart? I think that leaves me out. Unless naïveté will do instead."

"You don't understand what I mean by pure. It is not a judgment on your life. It refers only to your state in the moment of action. Purity is the absence of a gaining idea."

"Such as?"

"Such as, 'I did this, I did that,' " his guru said. "As soon as you think a thought like that, your spontaneity vanishes, taking with it your skill. You are left only with the ineffective gesture of ego. When you face a fight, your opponent can be defeated, but not by you."

"I'll remember that," Hob said.

As Fric advanced, Hob narrowed his eyes to slits, the better not to see trouble with. His body froze into the apparently awkward posture that presages the onset of sun li, the ultimate offensive. Fric came at him from the left, Frac straight on. Frac's bulk, backlit by the swinging overhead bulb spinning at the end of its white plastic cord, cast its shadow over Hob a split second before his opponent himself arrived. Fric meanwhile, shoulders hunched and knees bent to minimize his already inconsiderable height, his shadow, side-lit, looming taller than the man himself, scuttled toward Hob like a giant spider in an attack all the more deadly for its appearance of ineffectuality.

At this crucial moment, Hob's body disconnected from his mind. His head moved of its own accord, with a mincing delicacy, allowing Frac's swinging sausage arm to move harmlessly a fraction of an inch from Hob's head. At the same moment Hob's feet performed an economical little shuffle and Fric hurtled past him and banged hard into a wall and slid to the ground with a dazed expression on his face of a malevolent dwarf sired by a banshee.

Hob saw this only out of the corner of his eye, of course, since his attention was taken up with the larger and more formidable Frac. His little shuffle, while evading Fric nicely, had done nothing for him anent the trajectory of Frac's murderous onrush. There was time only, in a maneuver that will be sanctioned by the dojos of future, but is unheard of in this day and age, for him to thrust out his elbow, allowing Frac to ram his nose against it, and bringing him to so quick a halt that he was thrown back upon himself.

At that point, recovering his balance nicely, Hob pushed himself hard into the ponderous but momentarily becalmed Frac, the point of his shoulder impacting against the man's larynx. Frac blinked twice, his eyes bulged like peeled blue eggshells, and he collapsed in a heap in a manner reminiscent of reconstructions of how a brontosaurus would fall if it were to be shot in its tiny brain by a hunter from the future equipped with an express rifle and an insatiable desire for the great hunt.

Hob stepped back, a chortle rising to his lips. His enemies were down and out. "I did it!" he cried aloud.

At that moment, of course, the sun li technique failed him. His appreciation for his own cleverness, the inevitable gaining idea, blunted his senses. He did not hear the footsteps behind him, but knew later, in a moment of dry retrospection, that they were sounds that must have been logically present, since they were concomitant with the progress of whoever it was who got close enough to hit him across the back of the head.

It would not be incorrect to say that stars exploded in his

eyes. Hob found himself on the floor of the warehouse inching his free hand toward a shiny black object which lay conveniently close but could have played no part in his salvation even had he been able to reach it, since it was nothing but a galosh, and a worn one at that. Easy enough for Aurora to point that out later, when they were out of the mess. But how was Hob to know at the time that the black object was a galosh, and not a cosh? For that matter, how was he to know what was apparent to her from the moment of her return, gun in hand: that the screeching sound from above meant trouble for someone. For what should come plummeting down from the ceiling joists but a wheelbarrow full of pig iron in the form of large ingots, one of which missed Hob by no more than a foot, and another, rebounding off a rotting building member, ricocheted into Frac with sufficient force to remind the pasty-faced hit man that you gets no bread with one meatball.

Hob did realize that it put the hit man out of action, whores de combat, as they used to say in the Rainbow Division, and forced Fric, now solo, into an instant change of plan. The skinny hit man in the long black overcoat, looking like a truncated William Burroughs filled with venemous green Jell-O, slapped his partner back to consciousness, and they both looked surprised at Aurora holding the Luger on them.

"Take a gun, Hob," Aurora said.

Hob picked up one, noting carefully that the safeties seemed to have been released and the weapon was apparently in full firing position.

And then the two hit men had scrambled to their feet and were running, Frac huge and quivering, moving fast for a fat man on small dancer's feet, and Fric scuttling along beside him, a venemous small spider of a man, darting back into the shadows of the warehouse.

And then they were alone, and the city was silent except for the sound of a motorcycle coming down the street.

It was driven by a small man in a big leather jacket. The man was bald and had big ears. He dismounted, put the bike on its stand, killed the motor, and said, "Hob Draconian?"

"That's me," Hob said.

"Good. Harry Hamm phoned me. Said it was an emergency. I came here from Queens on my BSA. What seems to be the trouble?"

"It's all over now," Hob said. "You're late. But thanks for trying."

31

In Fauchon's office at the Quai des Ouvreves in Paris, Fauchon's telephone rang. It was Radon, the chief supervisor. "Fauchon, I've got a long distance from New York. A Mr. Emilio Vasari, special agent of the Drug Squad. Inspector, I have already spoken to Bureau Chief Pasquinod, who has urged full cooperation. He assigned you to work with M. Vasari because you speak English."

"Yes, I speak her a little," Fauchon said.

"I'll put him through now."

He waited. There was a clicking on the line. Then an American voice. "This is Emilio Vasari."

"What seems to be the trouble, Special Agent?" Fauchon asked.

"I'll get directly to it," Emilio said. "A woman is traveling by Air France to Paris tomorrow morning. We have reason to believe that either she, or, more likely, her traveling companion, an American, will be carrying a large amount of cocaine in their luggage."

"Unwise of them," Fauchon said. "Though the customs inspection at De Gaulle is frequently lax. Still, we can see to that. If you wish, I will call my colleague, Superintendent Grapneau, at the De Gaulle customs, and he will have his men search the luggage with especial care and arrest the criminals if your information turns out to be true."

"No, no, that's not what I want at all," Emilio said.

"You do not?" Fauchon asked.

"Certainly not. I'm not interested in arresting some mule, a carrier, I mean, which I'm sure is what this operation is. I want whoever they're delivering it to."

"And do you know who that is?"

"Strictly between us?"

"Oh yes," Fauchon said. "I am aware that I have seen no evidence yet."

"We believe they're delivering it to a Mr. Max Rosen. He's a model agent, and he's presently in Paris on business. We already have a few things on Mr. Rosen. He's flying over the two people in question at his own expense. They're leaving from his apartment. Although we have no direct evidence, I believe Mr. Rosen is going to make a dope sale out of this."

"You could be right," Fauchon said. "It's certainly worth looking into."

"Yes, but tell me this, Chief Inspector. Can you let these people through customs and then put a tail on them so we'll know where they go after they leave De Gaulle airport?"

"And when we reach the source, when they turn the alleged cocaine over to Mr. Rosen, or someone else, is it then that you want the arrest?"

"No, I just want you to follow them, learn who they're delivering to. I want to be in on the arrest. I've been working on this case for almost two years."

"I can understand your feelings," Fauchon said. "I will be pleased to greet you when you arrive. Will it be your first time in Paris? Do you have the police headquarters address? Good. Tell me the flight number and the names of the people."

"It's Air France three forty-two arriving day after tomorrow at ten-thirty P.M."

Fauchon scribbled. "And their names."

"Aurora Sanchez. And the man is Hob Draconian."

Fauchon cocked an eyebrow. "I beg your pardon?"

"Draconian. Shall I spell it for you?"

"No need," Fauchon said. "I know perfectly well how to spell it."

Later, sitting alone in his office, Fauchon wondered why Hob was doing this. From their previous encounter on the case of the missing sailboards, Fauchon had formed what he considered an accurate idea of Hob's character. The man might be inept, but he was not criminal.

The more Fauchon thought about it, the more disturbed he became. He had a liking for the feckless American. There was a sweetness about Hob that no attempt at being tough could conceal. So what was up?

After thinking about it for a few minutes, Fauchon decided to see what he could learn. He called Hob's friend and business associate, Nigel Wheaton, and asked him if he could drop into police headquarters for a chat. Nigel, all aplomb, said he'd be delighted.

32

Nigel came in half an hour later wearing an old but very well made tweed suit from one of the famous British men's tailors. Wheaton's beard was freshly brushed, his wild reddish blond hair was somewhat kempt. Nigel sat down in the straight-backed wooden chair facing Fauchon's desk.

"Coffee?" Fauchon asked. He pressed a buzzer without waiting for a reply. When Saucierre, the new man, poked his head in the door, Fauchon sent him down to the brasserie for coffee and croissants.

"That will be nice," Nigel said. "You're looking well, Inspector."

"Appearances are deceiving," Fauchon said. "I have recently had—what do you call it?"—he gestured at his stomach. *"Un crise de foie."*

"Liver trouble," Nigel supplied. "The famous French liver."

"Yes. Precisely."

"Sorry to hear it. Is there anything I can do for you, Inspector?"

"Oh, no, no. I just like to chat with my friends from time to time. Tell me, Nigel, have you been in touch recently with Hob?"

"Talked with him just a few hours ago. He's returning to Paris today, as I'm sure you know."

Fauchon nodded. "Is all well with Hob? Has he any special concern on his mind these days?"

Nigel looked at him, considered several lies, finally decided to tell the truth this time, since Fauchon probably knew it anyhow.

"Hob has a property in Ibiza, what they call a finca. It is a farmhouse and several hectares of land. Recently the mortgage on it fell due. Hob has been trying to raise money to pay it off."

"Is there a deadline?"

"Rather a severe one, I fear. July fifteenth."

"And if Hob does not raise the money?"

"Then he stands to lose the finca."

"Does it mean so much to him, this finca?"

"I'm afraid it does."

"But why?" Fauchon asked. "My understanding is that Ibiza is nothing but a cheap vacation spot. A cut-rate Miami Beach of Europe, *n'cest pas?*"

"That's very apt, Inspector," Nigel said. "But to some people, expecially those who came there in the sixties, Ibiza is something rather different."

"Different? How?"

"For many it makes a rite of passage."

"Please explain what a rite of passage is."

Nigel thought for a moment, then said, "In Anglo-Saxon countries everybody knows what it means when a group of men meet and spend an evening together pounding drums. That is intended to be a rite of passage. They want to belong to something."

Like many Anglo-Saxon things, Fauchon found this almost incomprehensible, but nodded anyway.

"We can assume that they haven't found anything to belong to, because if they had they'd be belonging to it already. Since they haven't found it, they're expressing their faith that it does exist, somewhere. That there's something worth doing. Something worth fighting for. Worth living for. Owning your own little farm in Ibiza is part of that dream for them. It is a way of saying, I am not a footloose wanderer with no home and no family. I belong somewhere."

"Interesting," Fauchon said. "And you think this analysis pertains to Hob?"

Nigel said that people like Hob had a lot of trouble trying to figure out what was worth living for. Home. Mother. Country. Those were the standard short list. For many people, including Hob, they didn't ring the bell. What Hob loved was Ibiza. But not the real thing. Hob loved his dream of Ibiza.

Nigel went on to explain that the Ibiza of dreams didn't really exist except as a sort of Platonic form, but that was what Hob loved. For him, Ibiza was the golden dream of eternal youth, of a better life, a piece of utopia for oneself. Not perfect, no; but its very faults gave it verisimilitude.

That was the best Nigel could do in the way of an explanation, and Fauchon knew he would have to be content with it. After the coffee arrived, the two men drank and chatted about the deterioration of Paris. That was always a safe topic.

Emile-Marie Baptiste Fauchon was born in Cagnes-sur-Mer. His father was a colonel of spahis in the French Foreign Legion. The family saw little of Jean-Phillipe-Auguste Fauchon during Emile's formative years. The colonel was stationed mostly in Sidi-bel-Abbès in Algeria during those years, where he was in charge of the quartermaster's depot. Fauchon's mother, Corinne, was youngest of the Labat sisters of the great perfume-making city Grasse. Fauchon lived his first ten years in Cagnes-sur-Mer. After his father's retirement the family moved to Lille, where Colonel Fauchon took on a job as principal of the Ecole Superieur. There, barring occasional holidays at a house the family owned in Normandy, Fauchon remained until he enrolled in the Polytechnique in Paris. After graduation he did his military service, which involved first a tour as a guard at the French mission in Tonkin, and then service in the French Police Militaire. By now Fauchon's preference for police and military life was well established. He joined the Paris gendarmerie soon after retirement from the service, and rose through the ranks to chief inspector.

He lived in a large apartment on the rue de Tocqueville in the Sixteenth Arrondissement, just down the block from the Ecole des Affaires de Paris. His wife, Marielle, was a plump, comfortable woman with lively black eyes who usually wore light-colored organdy dresses. Sterile due to an obscure birth defect, Marielle lavished her maternal attention on a one-eyed orange cat named Touissant and had a small but flourishing vegetable garden growing in pots on the roof of their building. She had inherited two small vineyards near Villeneuve-sur-Lot in Guienne and let them out to local growers. The income, though small, provided a useful addition to the salary of a French inspector of police.

Emile Fauchon awakened at 7:00 A.M. every day including Sundays, though he would have liked sometimes to lie in. Typically, when he opens his eyes, a cold clear white light fills the room: the logical, clear-sighted, slightly cold French dawn. He took care not to awaken Marielle, who rises soon after he leaves to take up her own daily round. This included shopping for dinner in half a dozen little shops on the narrow streets of her neighborhood; giving three hours a week to the Croix Rouge; and so on.

Fauchon's day took him entirely out of the *quartier,* by metro to the Fifth Arrondissement police headquarters in the place Malsherbes. The police building occupies the entire block and was an uninspired granite box with slightly incongruous marble columns designed and built by Herce in 1872. Within it was a warren of offices and corridors, with many different levels connected by staircases set in unexpected places. During the Nazi occupation this building's interior was hastily remodeled to serve as headquarters for the new Ministry of Mines and Harbors for the Seine and the Loire. Dozens of large offices were converted into hundreds of tiny ones. And when the police were given the place in 1947 for their new headquarters, it was found that the vast number of offices and cubicles was no more than what was needed to fill the needs of the bureaucracy, the infrastructure, the permanent cadre, the records division, and so on.

The duties of a special branch detective, as Fauchon actually is, could take him all over Paris, and even all of metropolitan France. The French allowed their officials considerable latitude in this regard, though any unusual actions and certainly any unusual expenses had to be justified later. It was the duty of special officers like Fauchon to be generalists whose study was not so much the individual crime as the ever-changing maladies in the body social. They did not necessarily go out on cases: they studied where and under what circumstances a case might have taken place. Their job was to be sensitive to the changing trends of crime. These special branch inspectors turned up at the snob bar of Closerie des Lilas and at the vulgar entertainments of La Cannebiere. You could find a special branch inspector sitting on a bollard beside the Saint-Martin canal, puffing on a pipe, perhaps, or cracking peanuts and tossing their shells into the oil-rainbowed water. Or he might be ordering a Tunisian sandwich at one of those little places off the boulevard Saint Michel, or strolling in deep contemplation in the Strangers' Wing of Pere Lachaise Cemetery, taking communion perhaps with Dupin, his spiritual forefather, not, of course, buried here, since he never lived, except in the only true sense, figuratively.

Inspector Fauchon would be less than human if he did not use his freedom of the city to take his coffee at a favorite café, and to show up for lunch at places that had found favor with him before. One of the serious amusements of Paris was choosing one's habitual restaurant. That was different from finding a good restaurant. One's habitual restaurant should serve pretty fair grub, of course, since someday you might have to bring your boss or your mistress. But you didn't look for gourmet food five lunches a week. Not if you want to get anything else done. Fauchon had simplified his intake. He tried to eat an omelette every lunch of his life. This was easy to do in Paris, where omelette making was one of the last great impromptu culinary achievements. Crisp and yellow, perhaps slightly singed around the edges, slid into a shoulder of the skillet and dotted with melted butter, with perhaps a little melted Gruyère in it, or some fried potatoes and a bit of bacon . . . Well, you could see the possibilities. Fauchon saw them almost every day in Les Omelettes d'Sybaris, a ten-stool omelette joint on rue de Racine just north of rue de Rivoli and boulevard Sebastapol. It was his favorite eating place. How convenient when it also offered some opening into crime, because then he would be justified in eating there every day.

In one respect at least Fauchon did not resemble your typical French police inspector. Others of his caste did not hurry, nearly every day, on feet made furtive by the irony of the situation, to a certain passageway off the rue Saint-Germain (fittingly named after that great mystic, the count de Saint-Germain, who, in the mid-1700s, fought and won several duels before it was discovered he was a woman and a mystic of exceptional abilities). Fauchon would go down this cul-de-sac until, halfway down, he came to a door painted a patchy fading blue, with a metal doorknob. This was always unlocked. Fauchon would open the door and go up two short flights of stairs. Ringing the bell that depended from a lanyard on the far end, he would wait, his expression saturnine and unfathomable, often smoking a Gauloise, sometimes tapping his foot impatiently.

After leaving the place of the blue-washed door, Inspector Fauchon would go back to work, and his daily round became more predictable. To La Petite Crevice in the rue Royale for tea in the English fashion and to wait out the first waves of the evening rush hour in which people milled around for several hours, going simultaneously to and from the center and the suburbs. Then he took the metro home to Le Grenouille, stopping, on his way, at the kiosk on the corner of his street to buy one of those small twisted cigars steeped in rum that the convicts used to roll in Martinique in the mid-1800s and which Regie Francaise, the national tobacco cartel, brought out in 1953 as Le Petit Curlienne. He would put the cigar in his breast pocket to smoke after dinner. And he would ascend to his apartment, where Mme Fauchon would have dinner already on the table, typically something high on veal and low on veggies. It would be going on evening, and both Fauchons watched an hour or so of television in the evenings. We have lost the notations of which shows they watched, but since France has only two channels and their shows are as like each other as pois in a poid it hardly matters. Whatever they watched was erudite, imbued with clarity, tinged with elegant irony, and utterly boring in a nineteenth-century sort of way.

And then to bed. Bed is indeed the inevitable conclusion of all our days, since most of us, those who sleep in the open under bridges no less than those who doss down in the mansions of the rich, are bound by the same circadian necessity to embark nightly on what Baudelaire called the sinister adventure.

The Fauchons' bedroom smelled pleasingly of lavender and patchouli. Sleep rounds out the day, wraps us in a cloak of forgetfulness so that we may forget what we did with the day, the innocent day that changed so utterly into the guilt-streaked night. And sometimes in the dark we roll over a little further than usual, encounter a familiar thigh or rump, and whisper, "Are you awake?" And hear the hoped-for reply, "Yes."

33

TIME AT LAST to leave New York. Hob and Aurora were sitting in the back of the limo. Kelly was in front, driving. It was 5:45 A.M. by the little dashboard clock. Traffic was light. A slight ground mist was blowing in from the Atlantic Ocean.

Hob's thoughts at this time were far away, in Ibiza. His mind was full of random images of Ibizan people and places: the view of the sea from the cliff at Sa Comestilla, Harry Hamm's scowling-cheerful face, Maria's sad beauty, and cut through these were images of the brightly clad hippies at the weekly bazaar at Punta Arabi, all of this interlaced with occasional real-life images of Aurora, silent on the seat beside him, her pure profile outlined from time to time by the tiny twinkling lights of the city as seen from the Van Wyck Expressway.

And cutting through all this was Kelly's voice, telling a story as he drove, the story of how good it had been to live in Manhattan before the days of the Knapp Commission, in whose prejudiced eyes long-accepted police practices suddenly turned into acts of deepest villainy, and an entire police force had to recharacterize itself by denying what it had done for so long. Someone had to swing for it, of course, and the man picked for that was Kelly, straight and true, who never ratted on his associates, not even to save his own job; Kelly, whose years on the force went down the drain when the Knapp hanging judges forced him out of his job and into the cruel world to find a new sinecure to replace the old one. Kelly's story was punctuated by any number of ad hominem devices like, "You know what I mean?" "You hear what I'm sayin'?" "I mean, what else was I to do?" And the like.

Aurora was wearing a nicely cut dark blue traveling suit by Givenchy, a big patent leather shoulder bag, medium heels. Hob had on his usual jeans, tennis shoes, yellow T-shirt with black letters across the front spelling out Bhuddaghosa High, and on top of it a dark brown tweed jacket with leather elbow patches of the sort writers are assigned to wear in the parade of similitudes called Earth where they demonstrate such things for the rest of the universe.

At Kennedy's international departures, Kelly double-parked the limo and carried the suitcases into the airport. A sleepy clerk at the Air France counter stamped their tickets, glanced at their passports, and gave them boarding passes, a ticket to ride.

"See ya around," Kelly said, and left them at the X-ray machines. They passed these without incident, and proceeded through the rest of airport security to the embarkation lounge. Here Hob just had time to read the front-page stories in the *New York Times,* while Aurora pondered chapter 7 of Gibran's *The Prophet,* and then the announcement came and it was time to board. They strapped in and soon the flight was under way.

In the enforced intimacy of the plane, with its dimly glowing little lights, its soft-voiced flight attendants bringing you drinks, its vibrating hum that went right through you and became a part of you and helped enforce the belief that you were in a time apart from all other times, a timeless time, in this timeless atmosphere of intimacy, Hob and Aurora fell inevitably into conversation, made all the easier because of a certain sympathy between them, all the more strong because unacknowledged.

Aurora spoke first of her life, how she had been born and raised on the island of San Isidro off the Atlantic coast of South America, not far from Aruba and the Netherlands Antilles. "It's a small tropical island, quite pretty, quite friendly, and—how shall I say it?—quite hopeless."

Her mother, Faience, was a primary-school teacher and she had ambitions for her children, pretty little Aurora and careful Caleb, four years older. Aurora grew up on the island, in a style of rural poverty known around the world, her father either run off or secretly dead, no one was sure, but secure among her many aunts and uncles. She soon became a tall, slim, pretty, light-skinned girl, at fourteen modeling for the island newspaper, winning a Lesser Antilles beauty contest at sixteen and getting an all-expenses-paid trip to Miami.

She found modeling work there without much difficulty. But she didn't like the scene. She had absorbed the American ideal of picking her own friends, and deselecting those who didn't please her. She wanted culture, which she had read about in school. In Miami, culture consisted of Latin dance bands and Central American poets. The music was great, but the poets turned out to be disappointing. At the end of a love affair she went to New York.

"I found work. I met some people. I met Max. That was about two years ago. And here I am."

Hob's life came up next, and Hob touched on the highlights briefly. Raised in a small New Jersey town. His father a life insurance salesman, his mother a librarian. Graduated high school, served in the army in Korea, after discharge enrolled in NYU. Not long after graduation, with the indifferent grades of a boy-man who doesn't know what he wants to do, he went to Europe. The picture cleared when he stumbled across Ibiza. His dream home. He spent the next fifteen years there and elsewhere in Europe.

And of course his finca. He spoke at some length about that, his problems paying for it, its various excellencies.

"It must be nice," Aurora said, "to love something as much as that."

"Oh, it isn't exactly love," Hob said, and was hard-pressed to explain what he meant. "I mean, yes, I do love the place, but that's not because it's so lovable, it's because it's home."

"We're alike in some ways," Aurora said. "You've elected

your own home. I haven't found mine yet."

On that high note they exchanged addresses and telephone numbers in Paris. And then there was a movie, and then there was breakfast, and then there was another movie, and then a doze, and after that, the announcement came: "Please fasten your seat belts. We land at De Gaulle in ten minutes."

34

THEY STUMBLED SLEEPILY through De Gaulle, 10:34 in the evening Paris time, passed through immigration and were waved through customs. Outside, in the big outer room, there was a crowd of people awaiting arrivals, and men in that crowd holding hand-lettered signs with people's names. One of those signs read, Hob Draconian—Aurora Sanchez. They walked up to the man. He wore a chauffeur's cap, but had on a tan suit rather than the usual navy blue of the professional driver. He was in his early twenties, with dark curly hair, stubbly face, prominent mustache. He had a large mole on his face, and there appeared to be something wrong with his upper lip, perhaps a poorly fixed harelip. He appeared to be an Arab, or perhaps a street apache from somewhere in southern Europe.

"Where is Mr. Rosen?" Aurora asked him, glancing around.

"At his hotel."

"Why didn't he come to meet us?" Aurora asked.

"I know nothing about that," the chauffeur replied in the Arab-accented tones of the Maghreb. "They simply told me at the agency to pick you up."

"And take us where?"

"To Mr. Rosen's hotel," the man said. "Or wherever else you wish to go."

"It's like Max not to show up himself," Aurora said. "At least he always sends a car."

They followed the man out through the airport's main doors. His vehicle, a rather battered Mercedes of some years, was parked at the curb. Hob thought about Kelly meeting him at Port Authority. Professional drivers seemed able to park where they pleased.

There was a man sitting in the front seat passenger's side. He was younger than the chauffeur, dark skinned, mustached, dressed in a dark shapeless suit. The driver said, "That is my cousin, Ali. I am Khalil."

Ali nodded to them vigorously. He scrambled out of the limo and took their suitcases, putting them in the trunk. He spoke to them rapidly, in ingratiating Arabic.

Khalil said, "He's saying he hopes you don't mind him being here. He likes to listen to the radio. He's just arrived here from Tamanrasset." Khalil rolled his eyes to indicate that Ali was either unsophisticated or feeble-minded, or, as is sometimes the case, a bit of both. They all got in the Mercedes and soon were speeding down the autoroute toward Paris.

35

IT WAS JUST past eleven at night. Hob watched the familiar highway signs come up indicating various destinations, most prominent of which was Paris. Traffic was heavy but moving right along, with a lot of heavy trucks from Belgium and Holland. In the front seat, Khalil and Ali were quiet, watching the road. The radio whispered Arab music. Aurora had her head back and her eyes closed. The car glided along hypnotically in a cocoon of swift-moving traffic. It was all very soothing, lulling, and Hob wasn't prepared for it when the Mercedes suddenly and dramatically accelerated.

Hob was thrust back into the seat. He struggled to sit straight and asked, "What's going on?"

Aurora gasped. Ali, turning from the front passenger seat, was showing a small blue-black automatic. It was not exactly pointed at them, but it was not exactly pointed away, either. It was ambiguous, like the scene they were in, but indications were on the sinister side.

"Be tranquil," Ali said, in accented English. "We have some company."

Hob caught color out of the corner of his eye and turned around and saw the flashing red and blue lights of a police car some thirty or so yards behind them. For a moment he didn't want to take in the implications. "Slow down," he said pettishly.

Khalil continued accelerating, then cut the wheel sharply to the right. The car plunged down the exit ramp leading to the boulevard Aubervilliers. Behind them the police car braked sharply and, slamming against the curb, managed to get into the exit behind them. Its siren was screaming.

They came out of the exit onto the boulevard at speed, causing traffic to pull sharply away from them as the Mercedes' horn screamed for track. A traffic tie-up ahead posed an obstacle that Khalil managed by pulling into the oncoming traffic lane, dodging oncoming cars like fixed obstacles and gaining a block on the pursuing police car. Then he made a wheel-screeching right turn, and then another. The siren was fading away. Khalil brought the speed down to an unnoticeable city level as they went on.

Aurora said to Hob, "What's going on?"

"I don't know," Hob said, "but at the moment it doesn't look too favorable."

"Pliz," Ali said from the front seat, gesturing with the automatic, "no talking."

They sat in silence as Khalil negotiated backstreets, coming out at last on the boulevard de Belleville, going past the North African restaurants with their couscous and their delectable tajines, past the flashing neon signs of the restaurants of a burgeoning Chinatown, and then into a backstreet and then into another, narrow, with houses flashing by on either side, and then a quick left and a right again into even narrower streets, deserted, streets without sidewalks or pedestrians to walk on them.

Khalil pulled to a stop in one such block.

"We will not detain you much longer," Khalil said. He had produced an automatic of his own. He spoke to Ali in swift Arabic. Ali got out and opened the passenger side door. He went around to the trunk, unlocked it, took out the pieces of luggage, and piled them on the sidewalk.

"Open them," Khalil said to Hob.

"They're not locked," Hob said.

Khalil snapped the latches and opened Hob's suitcase. Rummaging around for a moment, he pulled out a brown paper bag. Opening it, he withdrew a round burlap bag the size of a loaf of bread. Stenciled on its side was the legend Basmati Rice, Product of India.

"You always travel with rice?" Khalil asked him.

"It makes the perfect gift," Hob said.

Khalil gave a short snort of an unamused laugh and tucked the automatic into his coat pocket. He found a pocketknife in an inside pocket, opened it, and slit the burlap bag across the top stitching. When he had a slit an inch wide he pushed in a forefinger and withdrew it covered with a white powder. He licked his finger and smiled broadly.

"Yes, this is it," he said to Ali. "Give me the tape."

Ali took a roll of black plastic tape and handed it to Khalil. Khalil tore off a piece and sealed up the burlap bag again and handed the roll back to Ali.

"Okay," Khalil said to Hob and Aurora. "You can go."

They started to move down the street.

"Wait!" Khalil said. "Don't you want your suitcases?"

Hob and Aurora came back and picked up their suitcases. Khalil said, "End of the block turn right and walk two blocks. That will bring you back to the boulevard de Belleville. You should have no trouble finding a taxi."

"Thanks," Hob said.

"Don't mention it," Khalil said. He engaged the clutch and the Mercedes sped off.

36

Max was standing in the doorway of his hotel suite, dressed in a flowered dressing gown, smiling broadly. "Hob! Aurora baby! You okay?"

Tight-lipped, Aurora swept in. Hob entered behind her dragging both suitcases. He was arm-weary and disgruntled. He let solicitous Max guide him to an overstuffed chair. Hob collapsed into it.

Aurora looked around, unimpressed, and said, "Where's my room?"

"Just down the hall," Max said. "But let me get you a drink first. Rough flight?"

"Hob will tell you all about it," Aurora said, picking up her suitcase and vanishing down the hall.

"What's with her?" Max asked Hob.

Max was staying in a hotel suite at the venerable Hotel du Cygne on the boulevard Montparnasse. Although he had only been there a few days, already he was surrounded by the visual reminders of the great theatrical past of Paris: old billboards of Jean-Pierre Aumont in *The Blonde Sailor,* posters of Piaf, etc. Other names, other posters.

"Aurora's in a bit of a pet," Hob said. "She hates being hijacked."

"You're kidding, aren't you?"

Hob shook his head. "No. Max, we got held up."

"At De Gaulle?"

"Shortly after we left the airport. In the limo you sent for us." Hob described the events.

Max said, "I didn't send any limo. I haven't had time to set up a service yet."

"The driver had a sign with my name on it, and Aurora's."

"He didn't get it from me."

"He seemed to know who you were."

"Hob, think about it a moment. If I had set this up, would I use my own name?"

"Maybe not," Hob said. "Unless you were trying to be super clever."

"I'm not that clever," Max said.

"I believe you."

"What did you lose?"

"Not much," Hob said. "Just a small package of cocaine that wasn't even mine. Yours, I believe. About a kilo."

Max's heavy face had sagged. His pendulous lower lip drooped lower than usual. He looked like he had aged about ten years. He slumped back in his chair.

After a while he said, "Hob, about that coke—"

"You had Aurora or Kelly plant it in my luggage," Hob said. "I've already figured out that much."

"Hob, I can explain."

Hob smiled without humor, sat back, and folded his arms. "Go right ahead."

Max took a deep breath and let it out slowly. "Hob," he said, "I didn't set up this hijacking."

"But you did arrange for me to bring the dope through customs."

Max nodded. "First of all, it was perfectly safe. There was no chance you'd be caught at customs."

"If it was so safe, why didn't you bring it in yourself?"

"Safe for you, I mean. Not for me. And maybe not for Aurora. The fix was in, you see. That shipment was scheduled to go straight through customs with no complications."

"The question remains," Hob said. "Why didn't you carry it yourself?"

"I was afraid of a double cross," Max said. "You know Emilio, Aurora's boyfriend?"

"We haven't actually met."

"He's undercover Drug Enforcement Administration."

"Wonderful."

"It's what made this whole thing work. He wanted me to get this shipment into France. I was supposed to set up a sale, then he would bust whoever I was selling it to and get credit for exposing a big international ring."

"And you?"

"I was to walk."

"So it was all set up. All the more reason for you to bring it in yourself."

"Just one difficulty. Emilio is so crazy jealous at the idea of me and Aurora, I was afraid he might double-cross me and have me picked up. He'd lose his big case, but he'd have me out of the picture as far as Aurora is concerned."

"So why didn't you have Aurora bring it in?"

"Emilio is so crazy, we couldn't figure what he might do. Maybe he'd bust her out of sheer vindictiveness. You can't figure what a crazy guy in love will do."

"He could have busted me, too."

"Unlikely. He didn't have anything against you, and he knows you're not involved in this. With you or anyone else carrying, it'd be business as usual."

"I guess I don't have to bother telling you you had no right to do this."

Max gave a hopeless shrug. "I know, I know. What can I say? I figured the ten thousand dollars would smooth it over."

"Hand it over," Hob said, "and I'll see how I feel then."

Max looked more hopeless than ever. "Hob, I would if I could. But trouble is, that money was supposed to come from my end when I sold the dope."

"Max, what are you telling me?"

"I'm broke, Hob, that's what I'm trying to say."

Hob looked around. "This suite?"

"On credit. I was counting on this sale to get me clear. Wait a minute." Max got up and went into the adjoining room. He came back with his billfold. Opening it, he took out four crisp hundred-dollar bills, a fifty, and two tens. He handed Hob two of the hundreds and the fifty.

"This is all I've got, Hob, and I'm splitting it with you. Consider it an advance. I still owe you ten thousand. Now, I've got an important question to ask you. Did anyone know you were working for me?"

"It wasn't exactly a secret, was it? My associates, that's all. Why?"

"I'm trying to figure out who ripped us off. This hijacking was pretty obviously set up by someone who knew what he was after."

"It's more likely one of your associates than one of mine."

"I know that. I'm just trying to check all the possibilities. Look, Hob, could you do a little asking around?"

"You want me to find out who hijacked me?"

"Of course. You're a private detective, aren't you? I can't exactly put the police on it. And when we recover it, I'll pay you your ten thousand."

"Whoever ripped you off is not my concern."

"No, but I'm asking you to make it your concern. There's another five thousand in it for you if you recover it."

Hob thought it over. He suppressed his natural desire to tell Max to go take a flying leap into next year. That would leave him with nothing but an uncollectible debt. And the *traspaso* falling due in just over a week.

"All right, Max. But I'm going to need some money soon. What you've given me is about enough in Paris for a couple of dinners and a cigar. Nothing happens without money, you know that."

Max nodded. "I'll try to get a thousand together for you by tomorrow evening. Fair enough?"

The whole thing was damnably unfair. But there was nothing to do about it except go on. Like it or not, for the present at least, he was tied to Max and the stolen dope.

37

IT WAS AROUND midnight when Hob left Max's hotel and went out into the streets. He took the metro to porte d'Italie, and there walked to 126 boulevard Massena, where he shared an apartment with Patrick, an Irish flute player from Ibiza who was trying to make a commercial success of krillian photography as a way of predicting a person's character and future. Patrick wasn't in Paris now; recently he had moved in with a Frenchwoman and they were away visiting her relatives in Pau.

Hob entered the dark little flat. Patrick had left the refrigerator on, and there was a half bottle of white wine in it, along with some anchovies and some old chicken. Hob poured himself a drink.

The apartment, even with all the lights on, was as dark as his mood. The sounds of trucks penetrated from outside, big trucks coming from or going to the *peripherique.* There were four small rooms, one of them devoted to krillian camera equipment and special lights. The apartment smelled of cat and old pâté and fried potatoes. Hob put down his suitcases and looked around the cheerless place. Patrick had left the radio on. From it came a soft whisper of jazz, some sad woman singing the blues. Hob sat down on the cot that served as both bed and couch. It creaked loudly under him and gave way with a supple motion that presaged difficulty sleeping. He kicked off his loafers, threw his jacket across a chair. This place, with its bare lightbulbs and peeling walls, would have depressed him if he hadn't been so tired. He felt like all the sawdust was running out of him. Lying there in his clothes, he was on the verge of sleep when the telephone rang.

He staggered over and took it. "Hob, that you, old boy?" Nigel's voice.

"Yes, it's me," Hob said.

"Jean-Claude and I were going to meet you, but we didn't know what time you arrived. Nor what flight you'd be on, come to think of it. Forgot to write it down, old boy. Want to get together now? I can be up there in two shakes."

"Not now," Hob said. "Let's make it breakfast at Le Drugstore in Saint-Germaine, nine o'clock. Bring Jean-Claude."

"Righto, old boy. Everything go all right?"

"Not quite," Hob said. "I'll tell you about it when I see you. Good night, Nigel."

He hung up and lay back. He was trying to decide if he should get up and brush his teeth, which would necessitate unpacking. He was still considering it thirty seconds later, when he fell asleep, and it was the first thing he did upon awakening in the morning.

38

Next morning, Hob was sitting in the second-floor restaurant at Le Drugstore on Saint-Germaine, in a crowd of trendy people, most of them American, Japanese, and German, with an occasional French person around to lend local color. Hob was pouring his second cup of café au lait from the tall white pitcher. There was a half-eaten croissant on the plate beside him. Just then Nigel came hurrying up the narrow spiral stairs, with Jean-Claude just behind him. They slid into the booth.

"You look tired," Nigel said. "What happened to you?"

Hob told about the arrival at De Gaulle, the ride into Paris with Khalil and Ali, the hijacking, the meeting with Max afterward.

"I knew it!" Nigel said when he had finished. "I knew that sleazy bastard had something up his sleeve."

"If you knew, why didn't you tell me?"

"By the time I had sorted out the whole thing in my mind, you were on your way. Damn it, we even considered having you hijacked ourselves, didn't we, Jean-Claude?"

Jean-Claude nodded.

"Considered, or did?"

"We thought about it, for your own good, but we didn't do it."

"Nigel, are you sure? Because if by any chance you and Jean-Claude did arrange this, now would be a good time to let me know."

Nigel put both hands flat on his burly chest. "Hob, I didn't do it. It's clear that Max pulled this little trick."

"I'm not so sure."

"If not, who else?"

"That's what I hope to find out."

"I don't see why you bother. Haven't you had enough with this guy?"

"It's simple," Hob said. "I don't get paid until Max gets money for the dope he had me smuggle in. Nigel, I'm going to do it for the finca."

Nigel understood the sacredness of the concept. He had lost his own finca. Obviously it was the only thing to do. But where to begin?

"I guess," Hob said, "the first thing is for you and Jean-Claude to ask among your friends and informants to see if anyone knows anything. I can't very well wander around Paris looking for someone who fits Khalil's description."

But that was in fact what Hob did. After the three of them had finished breakfast, and Hob had described Khalil and Ali, and given Nigel fifty dollars to split with Jean-Claude from the money Max had given him, Hob took the metro to Belleville. It was ridiculous, but he could think of nothing else to do.

It did no good, of course. Half the population of Belleville looked like Khalil, and the rest looked like Ali, all except for the women, of course, who looked like Hob imagined their wives looked like. At least he got a good tajine out of it, and some first-rate mint tea.

39

In the meantime, shining lines of destiny that looked remarkably like the contrails of jet airplanes were converging on Paris. We can ignore all of them except those that came from New York, where the next strand of destiny's web that was binding Hob tight to Max was unraveling in the form of a heavy, middle-aged man of tough appearance, dressed in a plaid sports jacket and khaki slacks, who was disembarking at De Gaulle from Air France 170, a flight originating at New York's Kennedy Airport.

Kelly came through customs and immigration and caught a taxi. As he was getting into it, he noticed someone from another flight also getting into a taxi. It was Henry, Mr. Rosen's man of part-time work. Kelly didn't think Henry noticed him. Kelly didn't bother to holler.

In the taxi, Kelly gave the address of Max's hotel. Henry's taxi pulled out after him and he didn't see where it went. It occurred to him to say, "Fall back and follow that taxi," but he didn't have the French for it. Little did he realize that his taciturn, unshaven, dark-skinned driver was an Israeli, a former diamond cutter from Tel Aviv, who spoke better English than he did. But such are the vicissitudes of time, place, and plot.

40

Henry Smith sat there on the plane in the midst of the good-timers. There were 137 of them on this flight, the Louis Armstrong Paris Jazz and Hot Spots Commemorative Special. It was funny, him being on a flight like this, because Henry wasn't a jazz fan at all. Born and raised in the West Indies to the sound of tinkly deboobldebop and Rastafarian soul rap, he had soon acquired a taste, as unexpected to himself as to his family, for Ravel, Satie, and others of that ilk in the surrealistic Paris that haunted his fancies.

He sat now, reading his magazine, *The Black Israelite,* while others chatted and jived on all sides of him. He seemed to be the only one aboard who didn't know everyone else by nickname. That suited him fine. This was no fluff-headed pleasure trip he was taking. This was the big one, for all the marbles. When his seatmate, a large light-brown man in a beige suit with green velvet panels and a yellow-and-orange tie-dyed necktie, tried to strike up a conversation, Henry put a finger to his pursed lips. It didn't mean anything, but the man stared at him, bug-eyed, then turned to his seatmate on the other side.

That suited Henry fine. Silence and a little time for contemplation, that's what he wanted for this journey. He only hoped that Khalil had gotten his telegram and carried out his instructions. Khalil had been highly recommended by the Brotherhood, but you could never tell about Arabs.

The plane landed at Paris–De Gaulle at 7:10 in the morning. Henry disembarked with two light carry-on bags. He cleared customs and immigration without incident and took a taxi into Paris. It went against his frugal nature to splurge so, but this was the big one. Either he was going to come out of this rolling in money or he wasn't going to come out of it at all.

The sights of Paris came up around him as the driver entered the *peripherique* at Culaincourt and cut down through the heart of the city. Henry got his first look at Notre Dame as they came to the San Michel Bridge. Soon after, the taxi pulled up at the Left Bank address Henry had given, 5 bis, rue du Panthéon. Heart of Paris, baby. Nothing but the best.

It was almost 8:00 A.M. when he got out of the taxi at Khalil's address. Five bis was a narrow staircase between two big buildings. Henry passed many people on his way, most of them looking like students. There were quite a few blacks. Not that Henry cared. He wasn't prejudiced.

In the dimly lit hallway he found a button marked K. Ibrahim. 3b. He pressed it, waited, pressed it again, waited, pressed it again. Finally there was an answering buzz. The buzz continued, unlocking the front door for him, and then Henry was inside and starting upstairs.

The third-floor hallway was poorly lit. Henry had to flip his Bic to make out the door marked 3b. He knocked. A man's voice answered in French.

"It's me, Khalil," Henry said. "Talk American. I know you know how."

A moment of silence. Then the sound of a chain being withdrawn. The door opened. In it stood a tall, skinny, bearded young man in a bathrobe.

"Hey, man," Henry said. "It's me."

"You are Henry?" Khalil asked in accented English. Although they had talked on the telephone, this was the first time they had met in person.

"You got it. Gonna let me in?"

Khalil stood back and let Henry enter.

Within was a small apartment, dimly lit by the morning sun glowing orange behind drawn shades, and by a single overhead lightbulb. There was an unmade bed, from which Khalil had apparently just risen, an overstuffed chair, two wooden chairs, a table piled on one end with papers and books, on the other end with unwashed plates. There was a sink filled with dirty dishes, a small gas range, and no sign of a refrigerator or a toilet.

"You are really Henry?" Khalil asked.

"I sent you a goddamn picture of myself. Whattaya think I look like, King Tut?"

"Beg pardon, not so fast," Khalil said. "My English has not had much conversation."

"It'll do," Henry said. "You got my telegram?"

"Yes . . . yes." Khalil went to the table, rutted around among the papers, came up with the flimsy telegram form. It said, "Arriving tomorrow. Be there. Henry." Khalil showed it to Henry.

"Yes, I know what it says, I sent it," Henry said. "I never knew you lived in such a shit heap. This the best you could do?"

"I am a poor Iraqi student," Khalil said. "But I am a true warrior for the Cause."

"Hey, don't talk to *me* about the Cause," Henry said. "Ain't I flying here and breaking my hump for the Cause? The big question is, is you got it?"

"*Comment?*" said Khalil.

"The stuff, the caboodle, the question is, did you do what I told you to do or did you not?"

"I did what you told me," Khalil said sullenly.

"Any problem?"

Khalil shook his head. "One of the Brotherhood loaned me a taxi for the evening."

"And did you do it alone?"

"I thought better get assistance. I took my cousin, Ali."

"Can he be traced?"

"No. He left today for Algiers."

"Okay. And you got the stuff?"

"I have what you asked for."

"Then let's see it, my man."

Khalil pulled out two suitcases from under the bed. Behind the second one was the wrapped package he had taken from Hob's luggage the previous night. He handed it to Henry.

"Open it," Henry said. "That could be a package of curry powder for all I know."

Khalil took a knife from the table, made a slit, offered the package and the knife to Henry. Henry took out a little white powder on the end of the knife and snorted it. Soon thereafter, he smiled for the first time that day.

"That's it, brother! The real stuff! I'll just try another little poke. It's been a long night."

Henry took a second, larger snort and savored it for a moment with his eyes closed and head tilted back beatifically. Then he took out a little more powder and rubbed it into his gums. Then he closed the package and handed it back to Khalil.

"I just needed to be sure," Henry said. "But this ain't party time. Seal it up and put it away. You ain't been hittin' on that blow yourself by any chance?"

"I do not use the devil's powder," Khalil said scornfully.

"Glad to hear that," Henry said. "You and me put our noses in that dream bag and pretty soon there ain't enough left to sell. And selling it is the point of the operation."

"When are we going to do that?" Khalil asked.

"My man, I've come over to take care of that little detail myself. I'll tell you about it a little later. Right now, I need to get some shut-eye, then check out the lay of the land."

Henry leaned back in his chair, yawned, stretched, and looked around the room. He took in the clothing in piles on the floor, the books with Arabic titles piled in heaps beside them, the suitcase open on the floor beside the pile of books. The suitcase seemed to be crammed with dials and switches.

"What you got there?" Henry asked. "That some kind of communication device?"

"No," Khalil said. "That is my bomb."

"You shitting me?"

"Of course not. I never joke. It is what you call state-of-the-art, made in Germany of best materials. Guaranteed to blow hell out of anything."

Henry got up and walked over to the suitcase. He squatted down and peered at it closely, not touching anything.

"That thing is really a bomb?"

"It is, I assure you."

"Well just tell me this, my man. What in the name of twenty tiny demons in pink djellabas are you doing with a bomb on the floor of your apartment?"

"My instructions were to blow up M. Dourin, the minister of culture, because of the bad things he has been saying about our group, and his disparaging remarks about Islam in general. But I was told to postpone it to do this job with you."

Henry got up and returned to the chair. He shook his head in mock amazement. "Man, you try to blow up everybody what bad-mouths you, you got to put together a lot more suitcases."

"We don't expect to blow up everybody," Khalil said. "We just make a few examples. But that mission has been postponed."

"Then why do you keep the bomb here?"

"I have no other place for it."

Henry shook his head. "I'm going to have to do something about this. What if the police came around to check your identity card? Show me how this thing works."

"It is very simple," Khalil said. He moved to the suitcase, Henry following. "You see this heavy red wire? That's the locking device. The bomb is inert as long as that is in place. To use the bomb, you pull out that wire. That sets the mechanism. Then you have two choices. You can set a timing device here, by pressing this little button. Each number is a minute. You can set it for anywhere up to twenty-three hours and fifty-nine minutes. Or, you can press this big blue button here. When you close the lid, the mechanism is armed. When someone opens the suitcase, it goes off."

"Okay, I got it," Henry said. "Very simple, very nice. Don't even *dream* of doing anything with that while I'm here. I'll find a safer place for it. And for the dope, too."

Henry yawned and went back to his chair.

"Didn't get much sleep on that red-eye. I'll take the bed, you'll take the couch. That okay with you?"

Henry gave him the Big Bad Eye of Coercion, but it was wasted. Khalil was thoroughly cowed. He knew who was number one and who was number two.

"Yes, of course," he said, "I have to get ready for my classes." He started rummaging around for his clothes.

Henry sat on a chair and waited for him to get dressed and get out of there. The place was a shit heap, there was no doubt about that. But it was only for a while, until he got his hands on some folding money. But right now he wanted some sleep.

41

The telephone sounded and Max picked it up. It was the front desk. "A caller for you, Mr. Rosen."

"Who is it?"

"He says his name is Kelly."

"Just one minute." He looked at Aurora, who was seated on the sofa reading *Elle.* Covering the mouthpiece, he said, "Kelly is here. What do you think?"

Aurora shrugged. "Now is as good a time as ever."

"Send him up."

Kelly left his suitcases at the desk and went up in the little elevator, getting out at the third floor. There was no mistaking which way Max's suite was. Kelly could hear the voices from the elevator, Aurora's, angry, Max's, pleading. Kelly considered getting out of there and going around the block and coming back when it was all over, but what the hell, it wasn't the first time he'd heard Max and Aurora quarrel and he'd already been announced. He went to the door from which their argument came and rang the doorbell.

After a second or two the door opened. "Hi, Kelly," Aurora said. She was wearing black leather jeans despite the July weather and she was dragging a suitcase. She stormed past him and went to the elevator.

Kelly watched the elevator door close and the little openwork elevator disappear into its shaft. He shrugged, and turned to Max's door.

Max was standing there, apparently unaffected by the dramatic scene that had just gone down, his expression light, pleasant.

"Kelly! Damn but this is a very pleasant surprise! Come in, come in! What you doing over here in Gay Paree?"

Kelly entered and looked around. Max's suite was large and spacious. White curtains flapped in the mild breeze within opened French doors. The walls were covered with what looked like silk wallpaper and there were old posters of people Kelly had never heard of. The furniture all looked like antiques. The lighting was subdued and artful. It looked like a place a man could feel at home in while he planned his next move.

"This is nice, Max, very nice."

Max shrugged. "Just a place to roost until I get more permanent quarters. How about a drink?" He turned to the sideboard, where a group of glasses made small talk with three bottles. "Scotch all right? What are you doing here, Kelly? It's great to see you."

Kelly accepted a Scotch and water and took it over to a lyreback chair. He sat down, sipped the drink, and nodded appreciatively. He decided not to ask Max what had just gone down with Aurora. He said, "I told you, Max, I always had a yen to see Gay Paree. I told you that."

"Sure you did. But why now? By the way, I was going to telephone you. Some things came up and I had to leave a little hastily, you know how it is."

"Sure I do. Hey, I didn't take no offense, you not telling me you was going. You and I are square. You've been more than generous with me. I'm not here to put the bite on you."

"Hell, I wasn't worried about that," Max said. "You and I, we've always been straight with each other. If you need any help, let me know. I'm not in the greatest of financial positions just now, but pretty soon—"

Kelly raised a hand, palm out. "No, I meant it, Max. I'm not here to dun you for money. When you lit out like that, you left me without anything to do. I'm not blaming you, we always had that understanding, I worked for you as long as it lasted, and when you were gone, that was it. But I got to thinking. I'm serious about always wanting to see Paree. So I thought I'd take a look at the place before something else came up. And there was something else."

"Out with it, man," Max said, smiling.

"I know you didn't count on needing me over here," Kelly said. "But I thought you just maybe might anyway. No matter what line of work you're into now, it's good to have someone you can trust backing you up. Or run errands for you, like back in New York. Or whatever. Don't give me an answer right now. You may need some time to think it over. I'll be staying here for a week or two. We'll see what you think. If not, I'll go back to New York and no hard feelings."

"Well, that's really decent of you," Max said. "I will think about it, that's a promise. Where you going to be staying in Paris?"

Kelly tapped his raincoat pocket, bulged with a paperback book. "I got a guidebook here, my bags are downstairs, and I'm going out to find a place now."

"I'd put you up here, but you can see how it is. . . ."

Kelly nodded. "Oh, one thing more. You got a telephone number for that friend of yours, that Hob fella?"

"Sure I do," Max said. He scribbled a number on a slip of paper and handed it to Kelly. "What do you want to see Hob for?"

"Nothing much. He just seemed a nice fellow, and I don't know anybody over here except you. And I can see you've a lot on your mind. I'll be in touch, Max."

42

TWENTY MINUTES LATER, Max's doorbell rang again. Max went to it and opened it. It was Hob, looking creased and disgruntled.

"Why didn't they ring me from the desk?" Max asked.

"I told them you were expecting me."

"And so I was. Still. Come on."

Just then the telephone rang. Max answered it.

"Yeah, this is Max. Who's this?"

"Max, this is your old buddy Emilio."

"In Paris?"

"That's right, buddy boy. In Paris."

"Well . . . welcome to the City of Lights."

"Thanks a lot. Max, you and me, we've got some unfinished business."

"No we don't. This is France, not America."

"You ever hear of extradition?"

"What business are you talking about?"

"What I'm talking about I'm not going to discuss over the phone. I'll come by. But first I wanna talk to Aurora."

"Join the line. So do I."

"Don't kid around with me, fat man, I know she's there."

"Then you know more than I do."

"If I find out you're lying . . ."

"If you don't believe me, come over right now, we'll have some chili and watch French TV. I think there's a quiz show from Normandy on in about half an hour, ought to be a good one."

"All right. If you see her, tell her I got to see her. Is that private cop of yours, that Hob, is he in Paris?"

"He's right here."

"Put him on."

Hob took the phone. "Hob here."

"I need to meet with you," Emilio said. "You know a place?"

"Make it the Brasserie d'Italie, corner of avenue d'Italie and Massena in half an hour."

"Where the hell is that? Never mind, I'll take a cab. Okay. Give me back to Max."

"I'll be talking with you soon, Maxie. You and I got some unfinished business." He hung up.

Putting down the telephone, Max said to Hob, "That was Emilio."

"So I gathered."

"Do you think I should have told him about the dope being gone?"

"He's so smart, let him find out for himself. Max, what does he have on you?"

"About twenty years in a federal lockup unless I cooperate. That means setting up my contact over here so Emilio can arrest him and make himself look good."

"Are you going to do it?"

Max shrugged. "He's got me between a rock and a hard place. If I can't work something out, Mr. Y will have to go."

"I thought it's usually Mr. X."

"It is, but I decided to give him a different name. More refreshing that way."

"Take care of yourself, Max," Hob said. "Talk to you later."

43

"WELL, THAT'S ABOUT the stupidest thing I ever heard," Emilio said three-quarters of an hour later, as he and Hob drank beer in the Brasserie d'Italie.

It had become very warm, Paris finally giving up the unruliness of spring and allowing itself to grow warm and predictable. There were flower scents the air, too, for the dogwood trees were bursting into blossom.

The beautiful weather was wasted on Hob, who was having some trouble with asthmalike symptoms, and also feeling vaguely out of sorts and in no mood to hear a critique of his hijacking from Emilio.

The hijacking itself was having a delayed effect on Hob, a shock to his system.

At first, standing there in that backstreet in Belleville while Khalil pulled the bag of dope out of his baggage, dope that he hadn't known was there, Hob had felt nothing, or at most a sort of amused chagrin that he, with all his experience in this area, had permitted this hijacking to happen to him, hadn't anticipated it or at least the possibility of it. It was a numb sort of chagrin: he had felt as if he were wrapped in a protective sort of a grayness. But soon that gave way to a feeling of annoyance and shame that he, Hob, clever, sophisticated Hob, had not foreseen this, had not foreseen or figured out that getting ten thousand dollars for escorting a beautiful woman to Paris was the sort of dream bait with which confidence games are made. His own desire, or need, for a lot of money quickly had brought him to this tangled situation where he not only wasn't entirely sure of what he was doing, but was equally unsure if he even wanted to do it in the first place. At times like this, times of extreme self-repugnance, all motivations, all reasons for doing anything whatsoever, felt like they were hanging by a string.

The deeper insight was that there was no reason for doing anything. But this was the edge of the precipice of insight that Hob shrank back from.

He reminded himself that moods of nihilism soon gave way to moods of enlightened self-interest, thank God. Meanwhile he had this fool Emilio, with his beefy shoulders encased in a Micky Mouse sports shirt from Waikiki, leaning forward across the plastic-topped table and giving Hob the word from on high.

"Stupid or not, that's what happened," Hob said.

"Sounds like a setup to me," Emilio said.

"Clever deduction," Hob said.

"You got any ideas who set you up?"

"Plenty of ideas, no answers."

"I suppose you know Kelly is in Paris."

"Sure. Spoke to him earlier."

"And Henry?"

"I didn't know he was here," Hob said. "How did you find out?"

"I checked his name in the flight manifests. That Inspector Fauchon knows you, by the way. He helped me check out a few people. Any of them could have set you up."

"That's true."

Emilio looked at Hob and raised both eyebrows as if a great insight had just occurred to him. "Hell, you could have set yourself up."

"Sure I could have," Hob said. "I must have figured out by mental osmosis what had been planted in my luggage, and then telephoned from the plane to my gang in Paris instructing them in how to hijack me."

"It's a little unlikely," Emilio said. "But maybe I can make it fit. You're smart enough to have figured it out."

"That's the nicest thing that's been said to me all day," Hob said. "Too bad it isn't true."

"Spare me your wise guy bullshit," Emilio said. "I'm responsible for that dope you lost."

"Hey, sometimes even innocent guys get hijacked," Hob said. "It happens."

"Maybe. I just want you to know I've got my eye on you. You were involved in smuggling a few years ago in Turkey."

"Fifteen years ago. And I wasn't involved, nothing was ever proved."

"You just happened to be around when the shit went down?"

"Something like that."

Emilio stood up. "Talking to you is like talking to a bad sixties comedian." He brooded for a moment, then said, "You wouldn't happen to have Aurora's address, would you?" Hob shook his head. "I'll be in touch," Emilio said. He got up and walked out, leaving Hob to pay for the beers. It was a small thing, but in Hob's view it showed a striking lack of class.

Hob paid and walked back to his apartment. He didn't notice the gray Mercedes taxi parked third from the end on the rank at porte d'Italie and boulevard Massena. And since he didn't notice the taxi, he also didn't notice Emilio sitting in it, reading a *Herald Tribune* and watching Hob cross to his flat on the other side of the avenue.

44

IT WAS EARLY afternoon and time for a nap. Outside was brilliant summer weather, somewhat hotter than Hob liked. Inside Patrick's apartment, the stone walls and lack of windows helped keep the place cool.

Hob sat down, took off his sneakers, peeled off his shirt, which had grown clammy, and stretched out on the cot that Patrick used for a bed and that was kept always open and pushed back against the rear wall. The cot was hard and lumpy. Hob punched the shapeless pillow into a shape he thought the back of his head would like.

Detectiving was all very well, but even a private eye gets tired. Or if not every private eye, then Hob for sure. Hob was ruled by the energy in his chakras. When it was high, he felt like a world-beater. But all too often his chakras were depleted, his reservoirs hadn't recharged, his outlook had not freshened. At those times he was tormented by obscure doubts and misgivings that seemed to come from the very core of his being. He didn't understand what it might all be leading up to, didn't dare even whisper a possibility to himself, desisted for fear of undermining himself entirely, so subversive was he to himself at times, or, as his therapist used to tell him, "You're your own worst enemy."

At a time like this, a nap was imperative. Even five minutes' sleep could knit up the raveled sleeve of his frayed self-image.

Now, just as he was closing his eyes and wishing he were in Ibiza, and almost getting there in what might have been a dream, the telephone rang.

Hob stifled a groan and rolled to a sitting position, not a bad accomplishment for a man in his mid-forties with intimations of losing his finca.

It was Nigel.

"Dear boy, you know I wouldn't disturb you during siesta except that we've come with something of importance. Potential importance, at any rate."

"We?" said Hob. He always had the feeling Nigel was speaking for the royal family when he employed the royal we.

"Jean-Claude and I. Well, Jean-Claude himself, actually. But I insisted we should call at once."

"Important in what way?" Hob asked.

"For discovering who hijacked you. Really, old boy, did you think I called you with news about your Uncle Pete in Baltimore?"

Hob didn't bother saying he had no Uncle Pete in Baltimore. Nigel, for reasons best known to himself, but for a motive probably not unrelated to classical straight-faced British whimsy, had always insisted on the existence of this individual and inquired about him every time Hob came back from America.

"Who do you guys suspect?"

"Hob, it's not as simple as that. We don't have a name yet. But I think we can get one."

"Good work, guys. Yes, of course I want to hear all about it. I'll meet you in an hour at Au Pied Cow."

"Good," Nigel said. "Jean-Claude will run up a modest tab while we await you."

Hob let that pass and lay down again to sleep. The telephone rang again.

"Hob? It's Aurora."

Hob tried to muster up some politeness. He pulled himself out of the enticing pit of slumber and said, "How you keeping, Aurora?"

He meant it as a pleasantry. But Aurora took it seriously. "Hob, I've got trouble."

"I'm very sorry to hear that," Hob said, temporizing until his sense of empathy came back to him. "What's the matter?"

"Emilio is in Paris."

"I know. I just had a beer with him."

"He just called. He's trying to get me to see him."

"Tell him no."

"I did, of course. But Emilio doesn't take no."

"He's going to have to. This is France, one of the few remaining lands of the free."

"Guys like Emilio get their own way wherever they go. Hob, are you for hire?"

"Being for hire is what I do," Hob said. "What did you have in mind?"

"A little escort work. I've got to meet a fashion designer on the avenue Montaigne and I'm scared to come out of my apartment. I'm really not up for a scene with Emilio. If you could just escort me to the rue Montaigne, then pick me up again in an hour or so."

"I can do that," Hob said. "Where are you staying?"

"Four thirty-seven, boulevard des Ternes, in the Sixteenth."

"What metro are you on?"

"I haven't the slightest idea. Anyhow, we haven't time for a metro. Take a taxi, it's on me."

"You sure? That's the other side of Paris from where I am."

"Now's not the time to count the centimes," Aurora said. "Just ask the concierge for me. Come quick, okay?"

45

Hob told the concierge who he wanted to see and the small Spanish woman called on the intercom in her office.

"She'll come right down," the concierge said.

Hob nodded and went outside. It was a beautiful early summer day, without flaw and without character. Blue sky, fleecy white clouds. Traffic moving on the boulevard des Ternes in orderly fashion. Down the street, the Brasserie Lorraine was doing a brisk midafternoon business, its terraces full of well-dressed people. All was well in the upper-middle-class heaven of the Sixteenth Arrondissement. There was no sign of Emilio.

Aurora came out wearing a smart navy suit and a little toque, a thirties style that was coming back strong this year. She waved to Hob and came over. She looked good, rested, but her eyes were wary and she glanced up and down the block.

"I don't think you'll see him around here," Hob said. "I just left him half an hour ago in the Thirteenth."

"That man scares me," Aurora said. "In case you hadn't noticed."

Hob saw a free taxi and hailed it. Aurora gave the driver the address on the rue Montaigne. As they drove, Aurora kept looking out the window.

"You really think he's following you?" Hob asked.

"I wouldn't put anything past him." She sighed and dabbed at her eyes. "You wouldn't believe this, but he was so nice when we were first dating."

Hob nodded. What was there to doubt?

"I know he walks around acting like a tough guy. I guess he *is* a tough guy. But he was just so sweet to me. And protective." She thought for a moment. "Maybe that protectiveness was a tip-off. Maybe it was really possessiveness. But go figure!" She sighed again. "In a way, it was all Max's fault. He encouraged me to date Emilio so I could keep an eye on him."

"Why would he do that?" Hob asked.

"Emilio was making Max do illegal stuff, and Max didn't like it at all, but hadn't figured out how to get off the hook."

"What did Emilio have on Max?" Hob asked. "Or maybe you don't want to talk about that."

Aurora gave a little laugh. "Hey, you're my private detective, aren't you? If I can't tell you, who can I tell?"

"True enough," Hob said, deciding that Aurora definitely had a way about her.

"It was a dope thing. Happened about a year ago. Max's regular source dried up, and he made a buy from someone else. Someone with the highest credentials. That was Emilio."

"Any idea how Emilio got on to Max? Could it have been through Kelly?"

"No, Kelly never liked Emilio or trusted him."

"Good for Kelly. Go on."

"It was the second buy when Emilio nailed Max. Pulled out his badge and gun. Showed Max a little recorder on which he'd taken down their entire conversation. Incriminating, he called it. 'You're going to go down, Max,' he said. His voice was horrible."

"But Max didn't go down."

"No. He started to plead with Emilio, said he was just a user, a small fish, that this coke thing was the only illegal thing he'd ever done, that he didn't even lie on his income tax. And Emilio listened and nodded, and said, 'Well, maybe we can work something out.' And Max said, 'I'll do anything, just don't arrest me.' And Emilio said, 'I'll get back to you in a couple of days.' "

"And then?"

"About a week later, Emilio came back and told Max what he had in mind. He wanted Max to make a big buy, and arrange to sell the stuff. Emilio was planning to catch the people Max sold it to. And that's what's been going on ever since."

Hob suspected there was more to it than that, but he didn't think this was the time to push. There was also the fact that all this had nothing to do with him, at least as far as he could see at the moment.

The taxi stopped at the address Hob had given on rue Montaigne. Hob paid the driver from a thousand-franc note. They arranged for Hob to pick her up in two hours. She got out. Hob saw her safely into the Maintenon, then sent the driver on to Saint-Denis.

46

JEAN-CLAUDE AND Nigel were at a table on the terrace of Au Pied Cow. They were just finishing off pizzas and beers in anticipation of Hob paying. Nigel was looking very well that morning, dressed in a light tweed topcoat and trilby hat, his beard recently trimmed, his hair neatly combed. Jean-Claude was wearing his usual louche look, tight blue jeans with a studded motorcycle belt, horizontally striped red-and-white sailor's T-shirt, a cigarette drooping typically from his long thin-lipped mouth. Hob was glad to see his team looking so well.

Jean-Claude wasted no time. " 'Ob, I think I have a clue as to who accosted you the other night. I believe you mentioned that the man was an Arab, young, had a small mustache, and a big mole on his left cheek."

"Did I say all that?" Hob asked. "Okay, go on."

"You also said he had a harelip."

"I don't remember saying that," Hob said.

"My God, Hob!" Nigel said. "You're supposed to be observant! Attention to detail is supposed to be the sine qua non for a private investigator."

"That's just in books," Hob said. "Real investigators often miss the little details. If I said he had a harelip, he probably did. What about this guy?"

"Well," Jean-Claude said, "it's not much to go on, but I did ask around. My friends tell me this guy Khalil is a heavy hitter from North Africa or Iraq or one of those places. My friends think he's in Paris to turn a trick or two."

"But what ties him to me?"

"If I knew that," Jean-Claude said, "I'd have the case solved instead of merely having a strong suspicion."

"Well, it beats anything else we've got so far," Hob said. "Now, where do we find this guy?"

"My friends did not know. But they know someone who might."

"And who is that?"

"Her name is Mimette. She's a young lady from the provinces, Nantes, I think, studying to be a high-priced call girl specializing in Arabs."

"I didn't know you had to practice for that," Hob said.

"You'd be surprised," Jean-Claude said.

"I guess I would. Where do we find Mimette?"

"She usually comes to the entrance of the Beauborg about this time to get her fix."

That was only a few blocks from where they were.

"Okay," Hob said, picking up the check as was customary for a private detective conferring with his operatives. "And how do we know her? You ever met her, Jean-Claude?"

Jean-Claude shook his head. "My friends say we can't mistake her. She has green hair."

"Seriously?"

"Yes, seriously. She thinks it is the latest American look."

47

THEY WENT TO the fountain called Tranquillite and hung around for half an hour. Finally Jean-Claude spotted a thin green-haired girl of about seventeen, in a tiny black leather skirt and polka-dot bolero.

Jean-Claude walked up to her. "Mimette?"

"What is it?" the girl replied.

"Are you Mimette?"

"And what if I am?"

"We would like to talk to you."

She looked Jean-Claude up and down. "Well, I don't want to talk to you."

She started to walk on but Jean-Claude blocked her path. His voice, which had been neutral, turned to downright ugly. "You will talk to us, Mimette, or you'll be the sorriest whore in Les Halles."

"Don't you think prostitutes have any rights?" she said, but she didn't sound very confident.

Hob said, "We only need to ask you a few questions."

"And what about me? I need money!"

"We'll pay money for you to talk," Hob said.

"How much money?"

"How much do you usually charge for conversation?"

"That depends on whether I have to talk dirty or not."

"We don't want any dirty conversation," Hob told her.

Mimette thought it over, swinging her little black patent purse against her skinny flank. "You are journalists? Out for a ripe story? That will cost!"

At that point, Jean-Claude stepped in. "My girl, you'd better listen to reason. Who runs you? Is it Gilbert? Ah, I thought so. This is his district. Gilbert happens to be a great friend of mine."

"You really know Gilbert? Big Gilbert with the beady eyes and the big ass?"

"Of course I know him. We were in stir together at Amiens."

She looks at him respectfully, but with pique: a combination practiced by French whores, who were world famous for their attitude problems.

"All right, I'll talk to you. But am I to get nothing out of it? They told me I'd get rich in Paris. I just want enough for a little pig farm. I have an eye on just the one. . . ."

Jean-Claude interrupted. "We aren't interested."

"You're not? But I thought you wanted my life story!"

"Not a bit of it. We want some information about a man you consort with."

"Consort? What are you accusing me of? I'm an honest woman! I don't engage in politics!"

Jean-Claude sighed. "Mimette. Listen carefully. We will take up very little of your valuable time. But we need to know about a friend of yours. Don't make me get rough. I enjoy it too much."

"A friend?" she asked.

"A recent friend. A client."

Mimette gave him a guarded look. "Which one?"

"I am referring," said Jean-Claude, "to the Arab with the mole on his cheek and the harelip who might be calling himself Khalil."

"Ah," she said, "you mean the student."

"Precisely," said Jean-Claude.

"I made him a special rate," Mimette said. "Do you know, he comes from a tiny village in Iraq?"

"I had no idea," Jean-Claude said. "I thought he was a big-city boy from Basra."

Mimette laughed. "You've got that all wrong!"

"But not the mole, or the harelip."

"No, you have those right. And you didn't mention the knife scar on his left shoulder."

"True," Jean-Claude said. "But I'm glad you mentioned it. Now then, Mimette, just tell me where we can find him and you can go about your business."

"It's too early for business," Mimette said. "Actually, I came out for an aperitif. You wouldn't care to buy me one, would you?"

"We're in a rush," Jean-Claude said. "Some other time, eh? Now, where can we find him? And what name is he going by, by the way?"

"If you're his friend, why don't you know his name?"

"I'm not actually his friend," Jean-Claude said. "I'm a friend of someone who knows him. He forget to tell me his name."

"He calls himself Khalil, just like you said. He's got a little apartment over near the Panthéon. Number five bis, I think it is, rue du Panthéon. That's where he took me. I hope I'm not getting him into trouble."

"Set your mind at ease about that," Jean-Claude said. "On your way now, little one. You needn't mention our conversation. In fact, we have something for you." He looked at Hob.

Hob dug in his pocket and found almost four hundred francs, change from the taxi. He gave the money to Mimette.

"Many thanks! she said, and walked off.

"Oh, by the way, Mimette!" Jean-Claude called after her.

She stopped and turned. "Yes?"

"I think you'll have more luck with orange hair. It will suit you better."

"Really? But is it au courant?"

"Definitely dernier cri," Jean-Claude said.

48

Hob took a taxi back to the rue Montaigne, arriving at 2:25 p.m. Aurora had been waiting for him just inside the Maintenon. She came out, looking both ways up and down the street, then got into the taxi.

"How'd it go today?" Hob asked her as the driver pulled away.

"Not bad. Saw their latest line. May be getting some work from them."

"I thought that was Max's job."

"It is. But when I get a chance, I set up things, too. How'd your day go?"

Hob shrugged. "You know how it is. Another day, another dolor."

Aurora nodded. They sat in amicable silence as the taxi wended its way to the Sixteenth Arrondissement. Like an old married couple, Hob thought, and speculated on what it might be like to be married to Aurora. It was a more interesting line of speculation than the fortunes of the girl with green hair.

The taxi pulled to the curb at Aurora's address. Hob said, "Want me to see you inside?"

"No, I'm okay now. Thanks, Hob. I'm feeling a lot calmer. I'll call you, okay?"

"Fine," Hob said, and got back in the taxi. He directed the driver to the metro Ternes. It was okay taking clients around in taxis, but Hob was a metro man.

Inside her lobby, Aurora took the little elevator to the second floor. She unlocked the door and went in, locking it behind her. She went through the foyer into the sunny sitting room.

There, on one of the overstuffed chairs, reading a fashion magazine, was Emilio.

"Hi, babe," he said.

49

IT WAS TWO in the afternoon of his second day in Paris and already Kelly was bored. He sat in the little café just across the street from his hotel, drinking his third cup of café au lait with the waiters looking at him as if he were crazy. Well, piss on them. In America they fill up your cup when it's half-empty and they don't charge you for it. In Paris, they charge you full price for each cup and look at you like you were crazy if you drink more than one. Sure, it was a cute place, with its red-and-white checkered tablecloths and flowers on the table and a waiter in a tuxedo even in the morning. But he didn't like it. Kelly had found one of the saddest of all truths: There's a lot for an American to dislike in Paris.

But what really bugged him was that he didn't know what to do. He had come to Paris on an impulse, expecting to get something going again with Max. He'd been Max's right-hand man for nearly two years, and somehow he'd expected that to continue a lot longer than it had. It did no good telling himself he'd come over here not expecting anything. He'd been expecting plenty, and none of it was happening.

But there were some complications going on here. First, the dope. Kelly could see that this hijacking had Max rattled. Who had done it? Thinking about it, Kelly was sure that the key to the thing was the hijacking, and that had something to do with Henry. He'd seen Henry get off the plane at De Gaulle. The guy was here in Paris somewhere. But where? And what was he up to? Kelly decided that if he could figure out that one, he'd be on the way to putting this thing together, and making himself useful to Max. And maybe even doing a favor for himself, also.

Henry was the place to start. But where was he? Where would he hang out in Paris? Was there some place in Paris where blacks from New York hung out? A jazz club? But then he remembered that Henry didn't care for jazz. Which was weird.

The only thing Henry seemed to care about was his religious kick. The Black Jewish experience, he'd called it. His own private freak-out was more like it.

Then Kelly remembered that Henry had talked once about his shul in Paris. "I've got an affiliation with those people," he'd told Kelly. And he'd been at pains to point out that these were not white American Jews, for whom he had nothing but the deepest contempt. These were Israeli Jews who had a synagogue in Paris. Or who were affiliated with a synagogue in Israel. Kelly had never gotten it straight. And they had a name. . . . What was the name Henry had said? Something to do with wine. Port? No, sherry. Only not spelled quite the same. Sheri. That was it. But Sheri what? Began with a T. Tsouris? Tfilim? Close. Tefilah! That was it!

"Hey, waiter," Kelly said, calling over the tall, supercilious tuxedoed young man who had kept him supplied with coffee. "You got a telephone book here?"

It wasn't so simple, of course. This place had some kind of a computer, they called it an *ordinateur* or something like that, and you were supposed to get your addresses out of that. Kelly wasn't able to manage it, but after a while, with the waiter and the manager's help, and with the aid of a pen and pad, they'd found the name and an address for it. They'd written the name down for Kelly, because he could no more spell it than he could sing "Aupres de ma Blonde" in pig Latin. And half an hour later he was in a taxi on his way there.

50

"DON'T GET NERVOUS," Emilio said as Aurora backed toward the door. "I'm not going to get rough with you. All I want to do is talk. Okay?"

"Look, Emilio," Aurora said, "I'm just not up to a big scene now. Let's do this some other time."

Emilio shook his head. He was wearing a tan sports jacket that looked like it had been bought off a rack in some mom-and-pop clothing store in Brooklyn. Under it he had on a florid Hawaiian shirt with sunsets and ukuleles. His Mickey Rourke look. But Aurora thought he looked like an extra in a hood movie.

Emilio prided himself on taking on characters. Aurora used to like this one. Now she was wondering if she could unlock the front door and get out before he got to her. She doubted it, but she was willing to make a try.

But Emilio, slouched back in the easy chair, wasn't making a move. His voice was low and unexcited.

"Now listen to me, babe. I just got a couple of things I want to tell you. First of all, Max's goose is cooked. I know damned well he arranged to heist that dope so he could get around me. I'm going to come down on him so hard he won't believe how much time he's going to do. So forget about Max as your protector. That's finished."

Emilio paused and lit a cigarette. He looked around for an

ashtray. There wasn't one in sight. Finally he spotted a little cloisonné china dish and tapped ashes into that.

"The next thing is, don't think that private eye, that Hob, is going to keep me off. I eat guys like him for breakfast. You're on your own, baby, and you got no one but me. But I'm here for you."

"Whether I like it or not," Aurora said.

"Hey, come on," Emilio said. "You liked it fine once upon a time not too long ago. Or don't you remember?"

"I remember. But I changed my mind."

"So you can change it back again," Emilio said. "Look, I'm not shittin' you. You and me, we get along real good. You need someone like me to provide you with all the good things you've gotten used to since you left the family shanty back in Jamaica or wherever it was."

"San Isidro," Aurora said, "and we never lived in a shanty."

"Well, I bet it wasn't no mansion, either. Never mind, I come from the bottom of Bensonhurst myself. I'm not calling you or your family any names. I'm just pointing out that we're from similar backgrounds. We go together."

"I'll think about it," Aurora said. "Now will you please leave?"

"In a moment," Emilio said. "I just want to make the position real clear. You're going with me, Aurora. Or you're going to jail. You and Max were in this thing together. I've got plenty on you both. Max is a definite. You can cross him right off your active list. But you, that's something else. Think about it. You can never get rid of me. Stand me up and I'll send you up. Play along with me and you can have anything your little Latin heart desires. Oh, I guess I didn't mention it, but I love you."

"Nice that you finally got around to that," Aurora said. "Okay, you said you'd have your say and get out. Are you going to keep your word?"

Emilio stood up. He was a big man, and he moved with dangerous ease. He walked toward her, and Aurora shrank out of the way.

"Hey, don't get edgy. I'm not going to hit you. I swear I'll never hit you again. But I want you, Aurora, and I'm not taking no for an answer. You think it over. I'd rather you came to me of your own free will. But I'll take you however I have to. You got it?"

"I understand what you're saying," Aurora said shakily.

"I've left a copy of my key on the table there. It's on top of my address on a piece of paper. The agency keeps this place in Paris for us agents when we're over. It's plenty nice, over there in the fashionable Fifteenth. I got a view of the Eiffel Tower. And there's no nosy concierge to butt in. You'll like it, baby, it's got class, just like you. But it's also practical, also just like you."

He walked past her, unlocked the door, opened it, turned.

"You come over to me, baby, and make it soon. We used to make beautiful music together. We can do it again. Don't make me come for you, because in that case Poppa's gonna be plenty sore."

He gave her a grin and walked out, closing the door quietly behind him.

Aurora went to the door and locked it again. Then she ran to the couch and burst into tears. She cried for about five minutes, out of rage more than anything else. Then she sat up, found a tissue, and dried her eyes. She got up and went to the chair where Emilio had been sitting. The key was there, on top of a slip of paper, just like he had said. The address was on the rue de l'Eglise, in the Fifteenth, just like he'd said. She turned the key in her hand thoughtfully for a moment, then put it into her purse. Then she went to the bathroom to repair her face.

51

Afternoon naps were the worst kind to recover from. The telephone rang. Henry sat up, blinked sleep out of his eyes. Khalil still wasn't back. For a moment Henry didn't want to answer the phone. He had the idea no good things were going to come to him in Paris by telephone. Still, maybe it was important. He picked it up.

"Yeah?"

There was a brief hesitation, and then the voice on the other side said, "Henry? That you?"

Henry didn't know whether he should admit or deny who he was. Who the hell could be calling him?

"Who is this?" he asked.

"You know me," the voice said. "It's Kelly."

"Kelly from New York?"

"Of course."

"Huh. You been here long?"

"Not very," Kelly said. "But long enough to learn someone hijacked Hob of the you know what."

"Yeah, I heard that, too," said Henry. "Listen, man, I got a lot of things to do. You wanna give me a phone number, I'll try to give you a call one of these days."

"Well, no," Kelly said. "I don't think that's going to do. You and I need to meet a lot sooner than that if we're going to do each other any good."

"Now for sure I don't know what you're talking about," Henry said.

"Well, to get downright vulgarly explicit, I think I got a pretty good idea who took the dope from Hob."

"That a fact?"

"Sure is. But I don't think I should go blabbing about that to Max and Hob before I have a little talk with you."

"You're right," Henry said. "We need to meet. Where did you have in mind?"

"I'm pretty new in this burg," Kelly said. "The only place I know is my hotel and Notre Dame."

"I'm sure as shit not coming to your hotel. Back of Notre Dame in about an hour?"

"Why so long and why in back?"

"Long because I got to do something first. In back of Notre Dame so we won't have fifty thousand rubberneckers with cameras breathing down our necks."

52

Hob was awakened by a knocking at the door. He threw a raincoat over his shorts and opened the door. Standing there was the concierge in hair curlers, and beside her a uniformed policeman.

The policeman said, "Inspector Fauchon's compliments, and will you please accompany me?"

"What's this all about?"

The cop shrugged. "Inspector Fauchon will enlighten you."

The cop either didn't know what was wrong or, more likely, wasn't saying. Hob told them to wait a minute, dressed, and, under the eyes of his concierge and half the tenants, accompanied the cop out to a police car.

Hob was a little disappointed as they proceeded without siren across Paris, across the Seine at San Michel and around to the back of Notre Dame. Here a cordon of police kept back sightseers.

Streetlights were spaced about fifty feet apart along the path. To the left, about two hundred feet away, Hob could see the brighter gleam of police emergency lighting.

A group of police, both uniformed and plainclothes, were standing around with their hands in their pockets, rocking on their heels around a bundle at their feet.

A light rain, no more than perspiration from the swollen sky lit orange by the lights of Paris, had begun to fall. The sounds of the city were muffled, seeming to come from very far away.

As he drew closer, Hob could make out the stocky form of Inspector Fauchon.

"Hello, Chief Inspector."

"Hello, Hob. Would you see if you can identify this fellow?"

On the ground, under the police arc light, surrounded by the police, was a man-sized figure under a black tarpaulin. Fauchon grunted and one of the policemen drew back the tarp.

Hob bent over for a good look, but the face was unmistakable. "Kelly. I don't know his first name."

"When did you see him last?"

"Last night. We had a beer together in the place d'Italie."

"Tell me about him."

"I don't know much. He worked as a chauffeur for Max Rosen in New York."

"What is Mr. Rosen's address?"

"He's from New York, but he's here in Paris," Hob said, and gave Max's hotel.

"Do you know what Mr. Rosen is doing here?"

"On business, as far as I know."

"What sort of business?"

"He runs a model agency. Why don't you ask him?"

"I will, never fear. Are you employed by Mr. Rosen?"

"I escorted one of his models from New York to Paris. We arrived last night."

"Her name and address?"

Hob gave it.

"Would you know if Miss Aurora Sanchez knew Mr. Kelly?"

"I believe she did. But you'd better talk to her."

"Yes, yes, I know," Fauchon asked, somewhat testily. "Right now I'm talking to you. Do you know what Mr. Kelly was doing in Paris?"

"Sight-seeing, I guess. I don't really know."

Fauchon nodded. "I may have more questions for you later. You weren't planning to leave Paris immediately, were you?"

Hob shook his head. "Not for a couple of days. After that I'm going to Ibiza."

"The famous finca, eh?"

"If I've still got it."

"Contact me before you depart. You are at the address I have for you? On boulevard Massena?"

Hob nodded.

"Do you have anything to add at this time?"

"I have a question. How was Kelly killed?"

"Two gunshot wounds. One in the neck severing the left carotid artery. The other in the heart. Either would have proven fatal."

"Was he killed here?"

"The assistant medical examiner doesn't think so."

"How did you know to call me? Or do you come to me for any Americans found dead in Paris."

Fauchon reached into his jacket pocket and took out a scrap of paper. "He had your name and telephone number."

"I gave that to him. What else did you find?"

Fauchon raised both eyebrows. "You want to play detective?"

"I *am* a detective."

"That's right, I keep on forgetting. He had not been robbed. His wristwatch was still on his wrist. His wallet was in his left rear pocket. Which tells you . . . ?"

"That either Kelly was left-handed or he had a sore right haunch."

"Excellent. The wallet contained the usual American plastic cards, a few hundred dollars, and a few thousand francs."

"So robbery was not the motive unless he was carrying his real money in a brown paper bag."

"You're very quick. And there was this."

Fauchon took a plastic bag out of his pocket and took a card out of it. He held it up so Hob could read it.

It was a card for Schloime's Kosher Pizza on the rue Tesson.

Hob nodded. "It is unusual to find an American of Irish ancestry who is a kosher pizza aficionado."

"My thoughts exactly. You do not know this place?"

"I have not had the pleasure."

"I will question the proprietor, of course. I'll be very surprised if it leads anywhere."

"Is there anything else?"

"No," Fauchon said. "You can go. Unless you'd care to confess to this crime right now and save us a lot of trouble."

Hob shook his head. "Nice seeing you, Inspector."

"And you, Hob."

It turned out that Hob was to see Fauchon again sooner than he expected. The next day, around eleven in the morning, Fauchon telephoned him at his apartment and asked if he would mind coming down to headquarters. Hob got there in about a half hour, and was ushered through the grim gray building to Fauchon's office on the third floor.

Fauchon was direct, businesslike, and not unfriendly. "We took the contents of Mr. Kelly's room from his hotel last night, after you left. Nothing too remarkable, except this. I thought I'd ask you if it meant anything to you."

He handed Hob a green folder with a New York Police Department seal on it. Inside was a brief dossier on a man named Etienne Hidalgo-Bravo, born in Jamaica, naturalized in New York, age forty-four, occupation cook. No arrests in New York. A brief typed comment noted that Hidalgo-Bravo was believed connected to the Islam Armed Organization with headquarters in Borough Hall, Brooklyn. This group was under surveillance by the attorney general's office and was believed to be implicated in the Buenos Aires bombing of the synagogue in that city in 1992. Attached was a photograph of a slim light-colored black man with hair in dreadlocks and a short beard.

"Have you ever seen that man before?" Fauchon asked.

Hob studied the photograph intently for a while, then said,

"Give him a different haircut and lose the beard and I'd say that's Henry."

"And who is Henry?"

"Henry Smith. He was Mr. Rosen's valet in New York."

"What is his dossier doing in Mr. Kelly's possession?"

"I have no idea," Hob said.

"Was Mr. Kelly by any chance a New York detective working undercover?"

"I doubt it," Hob said, "though it's possible. What I heard was that he'd been cashiered from the police force in some scandal and was working for Mr. Rosen."

"It all comes back to Mr. Rosen," Fauchon observed.

"You should be asking him these questions," Hob said.

"I will, and thank you for the superfluous advice. But I can tell you in advance that Mr. Rosen will prove not to have left his hotel since he arrived in Paris, and will have witnesses to prove it."

"He'd better have," Hob said. "Otherwise he's in a lot of trouble."

"And this Henry Smith. Would you know where I could find him?"

"I wish I could tell you, Inspector."

"I will check with De Gaulle. I would as you say bet dollars to doughnuts he's in Paris."

"I'd bet with you on that one," Hob said.

Fauchon shook his head. "Anyhow, thank you, Hob. Have you been able to take care of the matter of your finca?"

Hob shook his head.

"Well . . . *Bonne chance.*"

53

"YES, OLD BOY, I'm very well indeed," Nigel said into the telephone. He reached for a Disque Bleu and found that his pack was empty. That was annoying. He hated to beg without a cigarette in his hand. And Quiffy was eyeing him from the far side of the couch. She wanted her kibble, poor thing, and so did Nigel.

"Aston, dear fellow, how are things in Belize, eh? Yes, it's Nigel! Humid and hot, eh? Just as always. Good, good! Joselito's bar still there? Many's the good conch stew I've had there. You must give him my love. Is the expedition going well? Pushing off into the bush any day now, excellent! Delighted to hear it! How I wish I were with you! Lost cities in the jungle are very much my line of country, as you know. . . . No, not a chance, dear heart. I'm stuck here in Paris for the foreseeable future. . . . *Les affaires,* you know, such a bore. Yes, it's rather humid here, too. . . . Aston, the reason I called, this is quite embarrassing, so bear with me. . . . The fact is, I need some money. Not for myself. I'm doing nicely, thank you. No surplus, as they say, but everything is going well. The thing of it is, I've got a friend, Hob Draconian, you've heard me speak of him. . . . Yes, the detective fellow. . . . He's in a bit of a bind what with his mortgage falling on him like thunder out of China to coin a phrase . . . and I thought you had that twenty thousand I was so delighted to loan you last year. . . . Yes . . . yes . . . tied up in equipment, is it? Of course, that's the thing of expeditions, isn't it? No, no trouble at all, I can turn elsewhere, I just thought if you happened to have it lying around . . . pray excuse me for even asking. It's just that I'd like to do Hob a good turn. . . ."

And in another part of Paris, in the back room of Le Chat Verte, Jean-Claude was saying into the telephone, after ten minutes of talk about mutual friends, "Listen, Cesar, you know that bit of land I have near Saint-Germain-en-Laye, where you wanted to put up a restaurant? Well, even though it's been in the family for ages, I decided why continue holding on to it? The fact of the matter is, I have a friend who is somewhat distressed for funds at the moment. . . . So I thought that I could make you a very good price for a quick sale, which would also give me the pleasure of advancing your desire to introduce the true cuisine of the French Pyrenees to the Paris area. . . . What did you say? Thais, your cook, has died of the gallbladder? My friend, I am desolated. But a replacement surely would not be too difficult. . . . Ah. The tax inspector! Taken everything? My friend, say no more. One understands the position all too well."

54

THERE WAS A knock on the door. Khalil said, "Yes, who is it?"

"Inspector Dupont, Immigration Service. Open up."

Khalil sighed and turned off the small black-and-white television. He had been dreading this visit, though his papers were in perfect order. But the French Immigration Service was known to be less than evenhanded in these matters. Still, there was no avoiding it, and he unbolted and opened the door.

A large bearded man in a tweed suit pushed his way in, followed by a smaller man with a thin mustache. And behind Nigel and Jean-Claude came Hob Draconian.

"Hello, Khalil," Hob said.

"I do not know you, sir," Khalil responded at once.

"We were not formally introduced," Hob said, "but you did drive us from De Gaulle airport several nights ago. You and your cousin Ali hijacked us."

"You are mistaken, sir," Khalil said. "I am not a driver. I am a student at the Sorbonne. Ouch!"

The exclamation was forced out of him as Jean-Claude drove a fist into his stomach and Nigel guided him to a chair.

"We are not going to have a long discussion," Hob said, pulling up a chair and sitting opposite Khalil. "You hijacked me. I'd know your face anywhere. Do you still deny it?"

Khalil glanced to his left and saw that Jean-Claude had taken a small folding knife out of a pocket, opened it with his teeth, and tested the edge by shaving some hairs from the back of his hand.

"Yes, yes, I did it," Khalil said. "It was crazy, stupid, I should never have done it. Sirs, believe me, I am not a common criminal. I am political, I do not engage in crimes."

"Just give back what you took," Hob said, "and we'll say no more about it."

"If only I could!" Khalil wailed.

Nigel had turned away and given the room a search. It was a small room with no closets. It took very little time to look under the bed and the piles of magazines. He looked at Hob and shook his head.

"Where is it?" Hob asked.

"I do not know," Khalil said.

"Peste!" said Jean-Claude, and he put an inch of knife into Khalil's shoulder and scraped along the shoulder bone. Nigel hurried over and grabbed Khalil's head, preventing his scream.

Hob, trying not to look as if he were about to throw up, said, "Khalil, you'd better tell us. No amount of money is worth what my friend is going to do to you."

"Listen to me," Khalil said. "I'll tell you everything I know. I followed orders. I followed the orders of Henry. You know this Henry? He sent me directions from America, he was spoken for by the organization, he told me what to do. I brought your package back here. Henry came here and he opened the package, he said it was cocaine, he left it here for one night. Then the next day he took it away. And he took my bomb, too! No, don't use the knife again, I'm telling you everything I know."

"Where is Henry?" Hob asked.

"Ah, God, if I knew I'd tell you! I don't think Henry is really a part of our organization at all. But he took the package and left. The package and the bomb. That was yesterday. He hasn't come back, he hasn't telephoned. I'm convinced I'll never see him again. And I never want to! That's the whole truth!"

Jean-Claude looked at Hob. "Shall we see if he changes his tune?" He gestured with the knife.

"No. Leave him alone. Let's get out of here."

"He could be lying!" Jean-Claude said indignantly. "I barely scratched him!"

"No," Hob said. "Let's go. Now."

They left, Jean-Claude muttering, "Calls himself a private detective."

55

IT IS POSSIBLE to get from the metro stop porte d'Italie to the metro stop Cite by changing at place d'Italie, and then changing again at Denfert-Rochereau. But it is faster and more convenient to go beyond Cite to Chatelet and then walk back to the Ile de la Cite across the boulevard du Palais, and this is what Hob Draconian did. Coming onto the island, the Palais de Justice loomed on his right, and across the street was the imposing Prefecture de Police. He turned left down the short rue de Lutece and came to the main entrance of the huge and forbidding Hotel-Dieu. Inside, he walked down a snuff brown and ocher corridor, past nuns with huge floating headdresses, and down two flights of marble steps to the basement. A blue-uniformed attendent directed him to the morgue.

"Ah, Hob, come over here," Inspector Fauchon said. Fauchon was standing with a little group of medical men. He was wearing a lightweight fawn-colored topcoat. It looked frivolous in these grim surroundings. They were just inside one of the holding rooms, where ceiling-high rows of what looked like great filing cabinets held the bodies of the recent dead.

Fauchon said, "Dr. Beaufordans, could we see the subject?"

Beaufordans, a small man with a black goatee, wearing a long white smock with a white cap tied to his head, gestured to two attendants and said something in a low voice. The attendants checked a list and slid out one of the long filing drawers, removing it entirely from the cabinet. They carried the drawer to a long table and set it down, and, at a nod from Beaufordans, slid back the cover. Beaufordans himself leaned over and pulled down the gray rubberized sheet.

Beneath it was the cadaver of a man, small, his skin colored a pale yellowish brown, his eyes closed, lying as though in sleep. Beaufordans gently rolled the head to one side, demonstrating the great gunshot wound, now completely dry, that had destroyed most of the left side of the head, including the ear.

"Do you know who this is?" Fauchon asked Hob.

"That's the man I knew as Henry Smith," Hob said. "Has he been dead long?"

"About twelve hours. The single gunshot wound did it, probably a forty-five-caliber weapon at close quarters."

"Where?"

"The Saint-Martin canal near the rue des Recollets. Not far from the Hôpital Saint Louis, but of course they brought him here."

"Has Mr. Rosen seen him?"

"He identified him earlier. I'm sorry to have disturbed you, Hob, but I needed a second identification."

Hob stepped away. Fauchon made a gesture. Beaufordans covered the body and the attendants replaced the lid and brought the box back to its place in the cabinet. Fauchon took Hob's arm and escorted him out of the morgue.

They didn't speak until they were on the outer steps of the Hotel-Dieu. Then Hob asked, "Do you have any idea who did it?"

"Nothing I am at liberty to say at present. Do you have any ideas, Hob?"

"I believe Henry had an associate named Khalil. Has he been questioned?"

"We are trying to find Khalil. There is an all-points bulletin out for him."

"He might be able to tell you something," Hob hazarded.

"We hope so. We'd like to know how he came to lose these."

Fauchon reached into his pocket and took out a plastic bag. From it he removed a string of blue ceramic beads with a silver clasp.

"What are they?" Hob asked.

"Worry beads, I think you would call them in English. Many Arabs, as well as many Greeks and Turks, carry them. Telling the beads gives them something to do with their fingers while waiting for fortune to smile on them."

"Where did you find them?"

"In Monsieur Henry's dead hand. Khalil's name is engraved on the clasp. Perhaps he will have an explanation—if we ever find him."

56

"HE WAS PRETTY stupid to think he could get away with it," Emilio said. "But he had us going pretty good while it was on. Still. It was just a matter of time. Am I right, Inspector?"

"You refer to Henry?" Fauchon said.

"Of course. It all ties into him. Especially with Mr. Draconian's recent discovery."

"And what is that?" Fauchon asked.

They were sitting in Max's sitting room in the Hotel du Cygne. Hob was there, looking sleepy, rumpled, and displeased. Max was in his dressing gown, and looked like he never planned to leave the hotel. They were all there except Aurora, and she was expected soon.

Hob said, "I ran down that matchbook that you showed me, Inspector. The one you took from Kelly's body. It was from a falafel stand in the Marais. I went to the synagogue nearby. The rabbi said that a man answering Kelly's description had been in looking for Henry. I told Detective Vasari about it."

"But you didn't think to tell me?" Fauchon asked.

"I forgot. I was a little too intimidated by the line of corpses you showed me."

"Only two. A private detective, in his line of work, must run across dozens, perhaps hundreds of such fatalities."

"You must be speaking of some other detective," Hob said.

"I would never have believed it of Henry," Max said. "Such a nice person. Religious, too."

"A double agent," Emilio said. "Pretending to be a Jew, but working for the Arabs."

"You still don't know who killed Henry," Hob pointed out.

"One thing at a time," Emilio said. "This is all conjecture. But it looks like Kelly got on to Henry, and Henry killed him. Then Henry was killed by his sidekick, this Khalil."

"Why?" Hob asked.

"How should I know?" Emilio said. "Maybe Khalil found out Henry wasn't really working for Islam. Maybe he found out he was an undercover agent for the Seventh-Day Adventists."

"Now we are moving beyond the realm of probability," Fauchon said. "Or so I hope."

"Pick up Khalil," Emilio said, "and the whole thing will unravel."

"At least to the extent that a case can be made against him," Hob said.

Emilio turned and glared at him. "You got somebody better in mind?"

"I don't have anyone in mind," Hob said. "And you still haven't turned up the dope."

"Khalil must have it stashed away somewhere," Emilio said. "There were traces of cocaine in his apartment. That's what you told me, Inspector. When your police find him, that'll tie it up once and for all."

Fauchon shrugged. "No doubt a case can be made. As for what actually happened . . ." He shrugged again.

"Well, it's enough for me," Emilio said. "Look, I gotta get out of here. I've got packing to do."

"You are returning to America?" Fauchon asked.

"To New York."

"What about the cocaine you came over to trace?"

"Hey," Emilio said, "that's probably vanished up a couple hundred noses by now. The trail's gone cold. Win some, lose some."

"You seem in a very great hurry," Hob said.

"I ain't got the rest of my life to sit around cafés drinking coffee like you do." Emilio turned to Fauchon. "I just have to pack a few things and I'm off to the airport. Inspector, it's been a pleasure doing business with you. If you ever get over to the States, look me up."

"You may depend on it," Fauchon said in frigid tones.

"Good-bye, Max," Emilio said. "Be good. I'm letting you off the hook." Emilio waved at them and went out the door.

"Thank God that man is gone," Max said. "Would anyone like some lunch? I can have the hotel send up sandwiches. Inspector? Hob?"

Hob and Fauchon both shrugged. Max reached for the telephone and asked in French for lunch to be sent up for four. He listened intently to a long, voluble explanation, then said, "Can you at least send up coffee and croissants? Great, thank you." He put down the phone. "It's some sort of holiday. The cook's away. But they'll send coffee. Hob, would you mind stepping into the bedroom with me? Inspector, if you don't mind?"

Fauchon shrugged again. He seemed depressed. Even his shrug was subdued.

"Hob," Max said, "things haven't worked out as we had hoped. I still owe you ten thousand. I can't pay it yet. But I can give you this." He took a billfold out of a little desk and took out four crisp hundred-dollar bills. "I'll get the rest to you as quick as I can. Okay?"

"Sure, it's okay."

"And no hard feelings?"

"I guess not."

Fauchon called from the other room, "Max, there is a person from the hotel who wants to speak to you."

"Just tell him to put the tray down anywhere."

"He wants to speak to you personally."

"All right, I'm coming." Max came into the sitting room, followed by Hob. A tall young man in a dark suit was waiting at the door.

"Good morning," he said. "I am M. Lenoit, assistant manager of the Cygne."

"If it's about the bill," Max said, "I'll be taking care of that later today."

"No, sir, it is not that. Though the bill remains a pressing issue."

"Then what do you want?"

"A message was delivered to the hotel. For you, sir." He handed Max an envelope with a BEA insignia on it. Max accepted it and the man left.

Max opened the envelope, took out a single sheet of paper, scanned it, then read it more carefully, then snorted.

"What's the matter?" Hob asked.

"Read it yourself," Max said, handing the paper to Hob.

"Aloud, if you don't mind," said Fauchon.

Hob read, " 'Dear Max, by the time you get this I'll be halfway to Rome. I made a deal with Maintenon to headline Ariosto's fall line. Sorry, darling, but this has all been very upsetting and I think we'd better go our own ways for a while. Thanks for everything. Aurora.'

"Huh," Hob said.

"I, too," Fauchon said.

"Yeah, and me as well," Max said. He accepted the piece of paper back from Hob, turned it over just in case there was something written on the other side, then put it on the coffee table and sat down on the couch again.

"The developments do not cease," Fauchon said.

"I wonder what next," Hob said.

And pat on the moment there was a knock at the door. The three men looked at one another.

"I'm almost afraid to get it," Max said.

The knock came again.

"Come in," Max said.

The door opened. A waiter came in with a wheeled cart on which were coffee for four, croissants, toast, and a single rose in a slim glass. He poured three cups and left.

"Comic interlude," Max muttered. "Coffee, Inspector?"

"Please," Fauchon said.

They sipped in silence. There was a lot of noise out on the street just then. Horns and sirens. They ignored it, waiting for something else to happen. And it did.

The telephone rang.

"Probably an announcement that war has been declared," Max said.

"Aren't you going to answer it?" Hob asked.

"I suppose I might as well." Max picked up the phone. "Max Rosen." He listened for a few seconds, then looked up. "It's for you, Inspector."

Fauchon got up, crossed the room, and took the telephone. "Fauchon." He listened for several seconds, grunting now and then to show he was following what was being said. Then he said, "All right, Edouard, I'll be over shortly." He hung up the telephone and returned to his coffee.

There was silence for a while. Then Fauchon said, "Aren't you going to ask me what that was all about?"

"None of our business," Hob said. "What do you think, Max?"

"I think you're right. Paris police business. What could it have to do with us?"

"Very well, I shall tell you," Fauchon said. "That was my subordinate Edouard. I had posted him to watch Mr. Vasari's apartment."

"Why did you do that?" Hob asked.

"There was something about Mr. Emilio Vasari that did not quite satisfy me."

"You want a straight line?" Hob said. "All right, I'll give you a straight line. What did your subordinate Edouard tell you just now?"

"Sorry, that's police business," Fauchon said. "No, excuse me, I only make the little joke. A joke in not very good taste, in view of what has happened."

They waited. Finally Fauchon said, "Edouard watched from his car as Emilio got out of his taxi and went into his apartment. It was on the second floor front. Edouard had a very good view of the explosion. It blew out the front windows. Mr. Vasari is dead. Well, it has been a day of surprises."

"Blown up?" Hob said.

Fauchon nodded.

"Do you mean someone planted a bomb in his apartment?"

"So it would appear."

"Well," Max said, "he was a thoroughly objectionable man. Not that I wished him dead. Khalil's hand is certainly in this, don't you suppose?"

"Why not?" Fauchon said. "We seem to have him for everything else." He finished his coffee and stood up. "I must go and see what I can see. Hob, can I give you a lift anywhere?"

"To the nearest metro, I suppose," said Hob, standing up. "What's all that noise outside?"

From the street they could hear a great blowing of horns and a sound of an excited crowd.

"It is just the celebration," Fauchon said.

"What celebration?"

"Bastille Day, of course."

"Bastille Day," Hob repeated. He thought for a moment. "Then this must be July fourteenth."

"That is when Bastille Day falls," Fauchon said.

Hob stood up as though an electric current had passed through him.

"What's the matter?" Max asked.

"I'm supposed to be in Ibiza tomorrow!" Hob cried.

"Is that the day of the famous *traspaso?*" Fauchon asked.

"Yes, it is! I gotta get out of here! Inspector, if you will excuse me . . ."

57

Just try to get into, out of, or around France on Bastille Day. Hob had Fauchon drop him at a taxi rank and he took a cab to his apartment on the boulevard Massena. He threw a few things into an overnight bag, grabbed his passport, and hurried off to his travel agent on the avenue d'Italie. His agent, Hassan, told him it was impossible to get to Ibiza today; it was not even possible to get there in a week, everything having been booked up months in advance. Didn't Hob know that Ibiza was the most popular destination in Europe, and Bastille Day the beginning of the great migration out of Paris?

Hob tried the ancient solution to all travel difficulties: money. He promised Hassan the four hundred dollars Max had just given him—fanned the bills out in front of him—and begged him to get him to Ibiza, or as close to there as he could, somehow. It was a matter of life or death. Hassan suspected it was more like an irresistible impulse, but set to work on the telephone, talking, arguing, cajoling, lying, threatening, charming, imploring—all the tricks a man will use to get his own way when there's money involved. Finally, by promising a friend of his at Cook's two hundred dollars—in addition to the four hundred for him—he got Hob on a chartered flight to Barcelona, with a place on a waiting list for room on the evening flight to Ibiza.

At Orly Airport they seemed to be playing an occidental version of the fall of Shanghai. Hob fought his way through the dense crowds of holidaymakers, bullied his way to the front of the line, found out the clerk knew nothing of his reservation, and refused to move until the man had discussed the matter with his superior and the reservation had been found. At last he got aboard the airplane.

On the two-and-a-half-hour flight to Barcelona, Hob had time to go over the state of his money. He had gotten $1,500 walking-around money from Max's apartment, $2,000 from Aurora, and two payments from Max, one for $250, and the last for $400. It all come to $4,150. He had given Nigel $50, then later given Nigel and Jean-Claude $100 each. He had spent close to $100 in Paris. Then $400 had gone to Hassan the travel agent, and another $200 to Hassan's friend at Cook's, and almost $200 for the ticket to Barcelona. That came to $1,150, leaving him with about $3,000. Not enough to pay off the *traspaso,* but maybe he could talk the lawyers into letting him pay part down, part later, or buying an extension, even a one-month extension. . . . Forlorn hope, but he had to do what he could.

Barcelona airport, and the usual summer madness. Here his luck ran out. The flight he was short-listed for had been canceled because of engine trouble. The next flight he could get was four days away.

Hob booked it anyway. The fifteen-minute flight cost less than a hundred dollars. Then he wandered around the airport, weary and unshaven, trying to think of something. And as he walked past a row of airport services, his eye hit upon the writing on a door: Catalan Air Services. Charter Flights Arranged.

Yes! He walked in the door.

58

The high-wing Cessna float plane came dipping out of the sunshine above the city of San Antonio Abad, second largest habitation on the island of Ibiza. It was a brilliant day. A hard northern wind was blowing in from Europe, driving out the famous mistral, scouring the land. It was a chilly wind, expecially for this midmonth weekend in July, just at the height of the tourist season. The people had descended on Ibiza this year in their thousands and their tens of thousands. From France and Germany they had come, and from England and Scandinavia. Nowadays there were even tourists from Russia and the Eastern European countries. Funny how everybody was able to afford a holiday in the sun. Odd that they had all chosen to come here.

It was middle European mating madness time. When the young of all countries pack up their lusts and journey to the Latin south, to Ibiza, with its sand beaches and its countryside scattered with discotheques and typic restaurants, to Ibiza, where the fashion scene ran nightly in the Old Port of the city, a place so picturesque that it would only be a matter of time before a series of nostalgic films would be made there.

Ibiza, where the air in July is electric with sex. Where the wine flows and the drugs gurgle. Where the art galleries roam. Ibiza, a place with many points in common with resort places all around the world, but absolutely unique, with its own mix of big money and low hippie style.

The float plane, droning in the air above San Antonio, began to descend in wide shallow turns. The beautiful bronzed people on the San Antonio beach didn't pay it much mind. There was a constant buzz of air traffic around the place, most of it big jumbo jets from Frankfurt and Paris and Amsterdam and Milan, bearing the seekers after pleasure. But there were also the little planes, because since millionaires had moved to the island, there had been a growing fleet of small-engine pleasure craft. The little seaplane did not belong to this class of airplane, however. It was obviously a utilitarian model, a worker of the skies, not a player, one of those planes that hire out from Barcelona, ready to take you to the Alps or the Sahara, wherever you wanted to go, with a minimum of fuss, ducking under radar, if necessary, because these sometimes carried the new mercenaries of the world, ready to take on any job, and not too particular on its being legal.

Yet the question remained: Why was this particular plane coming down over San Antonio Bay? If it was a smuggling run, they had picked the wrong time for it. Smuggling runs were done by night. What was it doing there, then? Well, consider: a float plane has to come down upon water, and the only water calm enough to permit a landing was San Antonio Bay. But that was not today, because that invigorating wind out of northern Europe was blowing up considerable wave action. Despite this, the ship descended to wavetop height, flying parallel with the deep water markers.

Twelve hundred was not bad, considering. But now he was there, and he found he couldn't get off.

"I can't do it, senor," the pilot said. "It's much too rough. I warned you of this possibility, remember?"

Quickly, before he could lose his nerve, Hob said, "Tell you what. You'll go down low and drop to stalling speed above the water, just beyond the beach. I'll walk the last couple of feet. Jump, I mean."

The pilot considered that, then nodded. "Yes, I suppose you could do that."

"Okay," Hob said, slightly disappointed that the pilot hadn't at least tried to talk him out of it.

Swimmers on the beach were suddenly rewarded with the unwelcome sight of a float plane coming in low and flat over the water, heading straight for the closely packed bathers.

Behind the beach there were a million dollars' worth of boardwalk stores and snack bars. If the plane missed the bathers, it seemed a good bet to take out some real estate.

Between the beach and the open water there were 568 bathers in the water, in imminent peril as the little Cessna came boring in.

Those nearest the middle of the plane's line of flight—where the worst swath would be cut should the plane continue landward past a certain limit marked by a line of white buoys—began to panic. They made shooing motions at the airplane. Moans and cries came from five hundred throats in seven different languages and sixteen distinguishable dialects.

The plane came on. It was a black blob with the sun directly behind it, coming in just above the water. Those watching saw another black dot, a smaller one, detach itself from the larger black dot. It fell to the water's surface. The plane meanwhile swept upward above the heads of the bathers.

After a moment's sigh of relief, the bathers remembered the second black dot that had fallen from the first one. Was it a bomb? Or had somebody dumped a body?

"I've got it!" a man cried. It was a body. A live, kicking, expostulating and spluttering body. A body trying to explain something to people who weren't prepared to listen.

The bathers circled him, shaking their fists, certain that this person had permitted himself to be used as a projectile in some crazy terrorist attack aimed at them.

Their rage and self-righteousness might have proven difficult for Hob had not a tall, dark, black-haired, black-mustached man with a small tattoo on his left arm and a badge fastened to his trunks put up his hand in an authoritative manner. The crowd fell back, not willing to transgress what might be the law with what might be an inadequate reason.

"I am a policeman," the man said. "Senors, please make way. I will take this man into custody."

59

Hob had never before seen the inside of a Spanish jail. That is not as much of an accomplishment as it might seem, because the Spaniards in those bygone golden days were slower than their fellow Europeans at locking up foreigners, perhaps owing to the famous indolence with which Spanish law suffered, combined with the argumentativeness of those whose job it was to administer it. Still, once they had locked someone up, they tended to forget about him.

Hob's stone cell probably dated from the Inquisition. A wooden frame bed. A single wooden chair. The stone floor, a dull red, and well swept. To one side, a small table with washbasin. A bidet. A window high overhead, too narrow to permit the egress of anyone but a midget with climbing equipment. This cell was in the old Fortaleza Prison in that section of Ibiza called the Dalt Villa. It was the highest part of town, above the Roman wall, above the Carthaginian and Arab antiquities. A clear hard bar of sunlight lay across one wall. The only sounds you could hear were the far-off cries of vendors in the open-air market far below.

Hob was doing nothing. He was just sitting. Hob had spent years considering meditation, and sometimes getting very close to attempting it. As a concept it appealed to him very much. He was especially fond of contemplating vipassanna meditation. The idea of studying mindfulness was very precious to him.

Hob adored mindfulness. He found it all the more desirable since mindfulness was a quality in which he was singularly lacking. Hob often tried to meditate in the many towns and cities he lived in, but always, the hustle and bustle of everyday life interfered with his efforts.

There was nothing to do in his cell. The police hadn't given him as much as a paperback book with which to pass the time, not even a Spanish newspaper. Hob couldn't quite make out the reason why, but he was to understand that their bringing him to the jail was not a formal arrest but rather a request for him to talk to them. He wasn't to consider this a literal arrest, at least not yet. The reasons for this strange behavior cannot be fathomed. Who can understand the actions of even one's own police? If their own motives are so often impenetrable, how much more so those of the Guardia Civil in a country with a divided soul, Spain of our sorrows? Perhaps it had helped that Hob had mentioned the name of his friend, Lieutenant Novarro, a lieutenant in the Guardia Civil, as soon as he was taken into custody.

Hob had reached the point where he could avoid thinking about any of that. He sat with his legs folded, in a corner, facing the wall. He had been sitting like this for almost three-quarters of an hour. His mind was blessedly blank. He was finally getting into the meditation thing, finally reaching the point where worldly concerns didn't concern him any longer. And then Novarro had to mess it up by unlocking his cell door and striding in with his black riding boots.

"Hob! What is this all about? Sergeant Diaz says you were dropped from an airplane onto innocent bathers in San Antonio Abad."

"I wasn't dropped. I jumped from a pontoon. And I wasn't trying to hit anybody. Quite the contrary. I was trying to avoid them, and I succeeded."

"But why? Why did you do it?"

Hob got up from the floor and stretched his legs. "Ramon, you know why I did it. It was the only way I could get onto the ground. And I had to get onto the ground because of the *traspaso.*"

He didn't have to say any more. On an island as small as Ibiza, not counting the million or so people passing through every year but counting only more or less permanent residents, everyone knew of Hob's difficulties.

"But Hob! You are already too late!"

"I'm not! This is July fifteenth, when the payment is due."

"Hob," Ramon said. "You were sent a notice. Since Saint Francis Xavier's day falls on the fifteenth this year, the date of your payment was moved to July thirteenth."

"They can't do that!" Hob howled. But his argument, he knew, was pro forma and entirely without merit. He had lost.

60

Hob and Ramon were riding together out into Ibiza's Morna Valley, sitting side by side in Ramon's gunmetal Deux Chevaux. They were running down the main road toward San Carlos at the northern end of the island. Just past the old silver mine, they turned off the main road and took a dirt track. It led between cornfields and vineyards. The vegetable fields were bare, since it was high summer. Each field had an *algorobo* tree planted in the middle. Along the sides, there were olive trees, very old, gnarled. Pine, *algorobo,* olive, almond, the trees of the Balearic Islands. They jounced along and the road becomes rockier and turned up into the central spine of hills that run down Ibiza's center like a ridge on a hog's back. Hob was amazed, not for the first time, at how large this little island was in terms of enfolded space. The place seemed endless when you traveled inland along the dirt roads that explore each turn and fold of land and connect every point to every other point and have done so since ancient times. Hob could never forget that Ibiza was one of the ancient places of the earth, where humans had lived continuously for thousands of years. Half the world had ruled this place, and then descended into the past to make way for the next. Various waves of prehistoric people. Then Iberians, Phoenicians, Arabs, Visigoths, Carthaginians, Romans, Catalans, and at last, Spanish. But the people of the island, the ruled, remained more or less the same through the centuries. They were a sturdy offshoot of the Catalan people, secure in their possession of the most beautiful place on earth. A place that Hob thought was now doomed to be trashed in order to stay in step with the rest of the earth.

They labored up the hills in second gear, and they weren't talking. What was there to say? And then they came into the curving track where Don Esteban's land began. They turned into it and ran along a drystone wall, then made a turn into the farmyard.

There were a number of vehicles there, including one taxi from Santa Eulalia. Someone must have paid plenty, because normally the drivers don't want to take their Mercedes-Benzes on these narrow difficult roads. Don Esteban's family was outside, sitting in the sun in little straw-covered chairs. It looked like a party. Old Don Esteban waved as Hob got out of the car. His two sons were there. They looked surly, but so far were acting polite.

Hob said, "Look, I know, I'm late with the payment, and legally I don't have a leg to stand on. But I've got the money. I've got it now."

Don Esteban said, "Hob, my old friend. Don't worry, it has already been paid."

"What?"

"By the beautiful young woman who said she was your friend."

"What woman?"

"She didn't give her name. But the money—that was there. We all witnessed it. Didn't we, boys?"

The two sons nodded, still surly. But Hob thought he could see the beginning of a tendency to accept him anyhow, since what was done was done and you might as well make a legend out of it. He could tell that someday he would become an honorary member of the family. Meanwhile, however . . .

"This woman. Where is she?"

"She might be at your finca, Don Hob. After all, she paid for it."

"I'll be back later for a proper celebration," Hob said.

And there was nothing for it but that he had to get right back into Ramon's car and they began sliding and lurching down the hill. They went back to the main road and turned north toward San Carlos and Cape San Vincente. Ramon knew the way as well as Hob. They hit some speeds and took some foolish chances. They went off the main road again and wound up into the hills. The 2CV slipped and slid and grunted and complained, but kept on coming. And they came at last to C'an Poeta.

61

Hob raced toward the door. He called inside, "Anybody home?"

Several people came out. There was Lonesome Larry, and Handsome Harry, and Harry's girlfriend, and the girl who was always hanging out with Harry's girlfriend. They flocked around him. But Hob had no time for them. Not yet. He was looking around. And then, there was Aurora, coming down the stairs, wearing a beautiful white dress with many things clinging to it and flying from it.

Hob said, "You paid my *traspaso?*"

"Yes," Aurora said.

"But why?"

"Max and I figured we owed it to you. Max had promised it. That was one thing. And without your help there in Paris, things could have worked out a lot worse then they did."

It was no place to hold a conversation, there in the *entrada* with Hob's houseguests gaping at them. Hob led Aurora to his own room, upstairs in one of the wings.

Paris seemed a long way away. But Hob remembered now, and said, "Did you hear about Emilio's death?"

Aurora nodded. "There's an item about it in today's *Herald Trib.*" She shuddered. "I won't pretend I'm sorry. He was a thoroughly despicable man. But I'm sorry he was killed. I wouldn't want to see anyone killed. I suppose it was that Khalil?"

"He's the prime suspect."

"So it seems. I hope he got out of France."

"Do you really think he did it?" Hob asked.

"Don't you?"

"Let's go back a few steps," Hob said. "There's pretty good evidence that Henry killed Kelly. There's evidence pointing to Kelly having traced Henry through his Paris synagogue. I think Kelly figured out that Henry was working for an Arab organization."

Aurora said, "It's difficult to imagine Henry as a terrorist."

"Oh, I don't think he was a terrorist at all. I think he was using the Arabs to help him hijack Max's coke."

"What a terrible thing to do," Aurora said.

"It must be distressing," Hob said, "to find a family member up to his neck in crime like that. I'll bet you didn't like it one little bit."

She looked at him wide-eyed. "What are you trying to say?"

"This is guesswork," Hob said, "but Kelly had some papers showing that Henry Smith's real name was Etienne Hidalgo-Bravo, born in Jamaica, naturalized in New York, age forty-four, occupation cook."

"Well . . . so what?"

"Aurora," Hob said, "Jamaica isn't far from San Isidro. I think if anyone cared to check it out, they could find that your family name was Hidalgo-Bravo, and that Henry was related to you. He wasn't your father by any chance, was he?"

Aurora hesitated for a moment, then said, "I guess you can find out if you want to. Henry was my uncle, my father's brother."

"And Max didn't know it?"

"No. I said he was a family friend from San Isidro."

"You helped him get his job?"

"Yes. But I had no idea he was going to—do anything like this! I had nothing to do with the hijacking! I swear it!"

"I believe you," Hob said. "But let's go on. Henry set up the hijacking, with Khalil's help. Khalil was an agent of an Islamic terrorist organization. According to Fauchon, he had a string of bombings to his credit. He was probably planning more."

Aurora nodded. "Then it's logical to think that he set the bomb that blew up Emilio."

"It's logical, but I don't think he did it."

She looked at him wide-eyed, waiting.

"I have to assume that Henry was in charge of the operation. The dope wasn't found in Khalil's apartment. I think Henry put it somewhere, a safer place. As long as he was doing that, I think he might also have hidden any bomb Khalil had in the apartment. I don't think Henry wanted anything to be left in the apartment, just in case something went wrong."

"It's very iffy," Aurora said.

"It was Henry's first time in Paris, apparently. Where would he hide the dope, and, if my supposition is correct, the bomb? I think he would call up his niece, the person who had found him the job with Max and had kept his secrets. I think he telephoned her and gave her the stuff to hold."

"Are you accusing me?" Aurora asked.

"I'm spinning a story," Hob said. "I'm just trying to satisfy myself as to what happened. I think that Emilio found you, wasn't going to let you get away from him. I think you saw how it was, told him you'd meet him in his apartment. I suppose he gave you a key. You went there, set up the bomb, then telephoned him and told him to meet you there. Then you put the kilo in your handbag and got out of Paris. Am I right?"

"Oh, Hob," Aurora said.

"I know it's unpleasant," Hob said. "But I wish you'd tell me."

"You're pretty close," Aurora said. "Except that I didn't take the kilo out of Paris. I got it back to Max, and he sold it like he'd been planning to do. My walkout on him was staged for your benefit. So you wouldn't think we were working together. He paid me fifty percent of what he got. And I came down here and paid off your *traspaso.* Max put up half the money and I put up the other half. So now what?"

"Now," Hob said, "I think it's time for a drink. And then some dinner."

"And then?"

"Ibiza is a lovely island," Hob said, "and I have the finest finca on it. I suggest you spend the summer here with me. You haven't lived until you've spent a summer in Ibiza."

Aurora laughed, a relieved laugh. "Hob, I'm afraid I can't spend the summer. But I'd like to spend a week with you. After that, I have to get to Rome. There's work to be done setting up my fall fashion show."

"And Max will be there?"

"Of course. He set up the deal with Maintenon."

"A week in Ibiza is better than a lifetime anywhere else," Hob said.

"I'll have to judge that for myself," Aurora said. "You're not going to mention this to Fauchon, are you?"

"Blowing up Emilio is no crime in my book," Hob said.